Call to a Quest

By Matthew Randolph

Cover Art and Design by Matthew Randolph.

ISBN 978-1-684-71302-8

Second Young Authors Press Paperback Edition, 2021

A Call to a Quest

By Matthew Randolph

Young Authors Press
Bay Area California

Warning:

This story was created by an introvert who at the time was suffering from monophobia because he couldn't see his friends during the 2020 Pandemic. This book is to make up for lost times and to help this individual process being lonely. He misses his friends. Especially the friends that helped create these characters through the role-playing game *Dungeons and Dragons*. He hopes he can hug someone in the outside world soon (even if it's a random person in the subway or something), and help him get over his loneliness.

Dedication:

This book is dedicated to my Mom, who taught me the Hero's Journey, My Grandfather, who reads so many books with me, and my friends who helped encourage me.

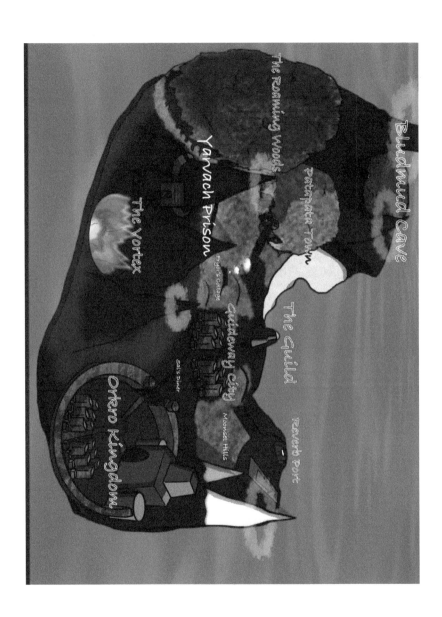

7

Table of Contents

The Quest

Nightshade Inn was as normal as it could be. The sound of the tavern at night, the jolly ogres chatting, the drunken dwarves yelling, and the beer reverberating on the wooden tables was all normal, until midnight. A stranger in a hood with a pendant around his neck opened the doors and strode through the crowd of the many species as they continued their chatting and singing. The bartender was the first to notice something was off about the visitor, for when he ordered his beer he said it in a voice as sharp as a knife, and when he went to reach out, the jug seemed to move through the air into his hands, cold as ice.

Once the visitor had finished his beer he thanked the bartender and gave him his payment. Then he strode over to the doors and reached out to the quest board. The quest board had been installed for anyone to post their troubles or outlaw notices. The stranger attached a slip of paper to the board and left as quickly as he had entered.

Ivan had only taken one sip of his beer before the sun appeared over the horizon, bringing another glorious day to Guidway city. He was a thin man with many flaws, but none of them mattered much to him. What he did have that were as near to gifts as could be were his sword, Tri-blade, a three-pointed sword made of unbreakable steel, and his friends. Grog, an orc chef, was an outcast from his kingdom because he preferred to cook with the women instead of fighting with the men. His second friend, Eioffrey, was a human like him, but was raised by Halflings. He was only ten, but was already the size of two Halflings his age stacked upon each other. He sought out no violence, but instead seeked the ways of magic from his village elder. Both of them now entered the door of Nightshade Inn, and approached the table Ivan sat at.

Once they sat down and pulled out some chairs, the Bartender came rushing toward them, checklist ready.

"May I take your orders, gentlemen?" he said, pulling out his pencil.

Ivan raised his beer cup, suddenly empty. "A refill."

The Bartender took the jug and turned to Eioffrey and Grog.

Grog gave a smile and said "I'll just take some beer."

"I'll have some juice, thanks," said Eioffrey.

The Bartender scribbled their orders down and turned away, but Ivan caught his shoulder before he could leave.

"There been any new posts?" he whispered in a quiet tone. "You know how much I hate it when others get at new missions before I do."

The Bartender turned and replied: "Actually, yes. There was a strange man who came in last night, ordered a jug, then put a slip of paper on the board. Should be somewhere in the middle," Then he turned to leave, for there were dishes that needed scrubbing.

Ivan got up from his chair and walked over to the board and snatched off the only piece of paper attached. He returned to the table and slid back into his chair.

"What does it say?" Eioffrey inquired.

Ivan read aloud: *"For whoever this reaches, I need help. I was adventuring in Bludmud cave with my crew and we got attacked. When I woke up, my friends were gone and I had been badly wounded. Please find them, and bring them to Farlam Village, as I am too weak to rescue them myself."*

Ivan rolled up the paper just as the Bartender returned with their orders. "But Farlam's an island away!" Eioffrey complained. "It's on a whole other continent! And supposing we even find this person's friends, we'll need passports to cross to Farlam, and you know how much those costs!"

"It doesn't matter. My sword and I can easily do this by ourselves," Ivan said.

"I highly doubt that," Eioffrey said. "You brag about your sword too much anyway. We all are coming on this quest,"

"Look, we missed something. 2000 Parvs is the reward. I think that's more than enough to cover the passports for the three of us," Grog said.

"Let me see that," Ivan said, snatching the paper from Grog's grasp. Pulling it to his eyes.

"Huh, it really is," he said, laying it on the table.

"So," said Eioffrey, "To Bludmud it is."

After the long and tiring journey to Bludmud cave, which was miles away from their little cottage in Guidway City, Ivan had started to have his doubts. He was confident at first, but now that the cavern was right in front of him, the darkness casting a menacing shadow across the ground in front of him, it gave him a chilling feeling, as cold as ice.

Eioffrey peeked over Ivan's shoulder.

"Ivan?" he said, with a worried tone in his voice.

Ivan looked at Eioffrey quickly. "Yeah?" he said, still shaking.

"You okay?" Grog said.

Ivan looked at Grog. "Y-yeah. Sure," he said, clutching his sword. "Come on, let's go."

As they entered the cave, Eioffrey held his pendant, and it shone, casting a light across the cave. Proceeding with a light, they strode into the darkness.

So far, they were halfway into the cave, and there was no sign of other Humans, Elves, Ogres, Halflings, or any other creatures besides the occasional scorpion or slug. The cave itself was a murky one, constantly dripping and smelling of mildew. Some parts of the cave were moist and foggy, while others were filled with crystals that emitted a bright, fluorescent blue. The trio was getting tired, and were especially bored.

"I wish we at least ran into, like, a baby Wurm or something. Wurms put up at least some kind of a fight. They're huge," said Grog, wiping the sweat off his head. "Or even, if we're lucky, a Blight. You know, little twig dudes."

"I'm sure we'll run into something soon," said Eioffrey. "Who knows, we might get to fight a Gelatinous Cube!" And chuckled to himself.

They passed into a corridor and observed it. The ground seemed to have been swept clean of any dust or grime, not a single spiderweb in sight.

Grog looked concerned. "Why is this hall so... *clean*?"

Eioffrey bent down and examined the ground. He wiped his finger on the rugged earth, expecting dust. No dust, and his hand was as clean as before.

"It's *too* clean."

There was an eerie squelching sound coming towards them, from the other side of the distant hall. The trio froze.

"I think we got a little *too* lucky."

The sound of slime and wet, dripping ooze came closer.

It was a Gelatinous Cube.

It was coming. Fast. It was no wonder the hall was so clean. Everything a Gelatinous Cube touches, it sucks in, and dissolves.

"We need to run!" Eioffrey yelled.

"Don't need to tell me twice!" Grog yelled back.

The three got up and started sprinting back to the way they had come. They ran until they came to a fork in the road, and stopped. Panting, they looked behind themselves.

"Where do we go?" yelled Grog, looking back at the advancing Cube.

Ivan pointed randomly to one of the tunnels. "That one!" he yelled. Just as they all advanced to the tunnel, another Gelatinous Cube emerged from it. Grog and Ivan almost fell into it, but Eioffrey summoned a hand out of the energy from his pendant and yanked both of them out of the way.

"React quickly!" Eioffrey yelled. "Gelatinous Cubes could come from anywhere!" Just as if on cue, another Gelatinous Cube emerged from the other tunnel. Still holding Ivan and Grog with his enlarged energy hand, Eioffrey dashed through the third tunnel.

Behind them, the Gelatinous Cubes coming from all the other tunnels slammed into each other with a squelching sound and merged together.

The three kept on running down the passage until they came to a steel door. Eioffrey dropped Ivan and Grog on the ground and reached out to the door, pulling it clean out and rushing in. Grog and Ivan quickly got up and followed Eioffrey just as he slammed the door back in place.

They turned to keep running, but right in front of them was a giant grid on the ground, covered in squares, which lit up with a blue, luminescent light, which faded quickly.

"It's a puzzle!" Eioffrey yelled. "We need to figure out the message. Usually these puzzles have pictures that stand for letters. We need to find out what it says!"

He pointed to a tile, which had a picture of a Torch. "That's T," he said. He pointed to another, with a picture of an Orc. "O."

"What happens if we touch the wrong one?" Grog asked.

Eioffrey broke off a long angular rock and poked a tile with a picture of a Mage. "M."

The rock tapped the tile, which lit up red, then the rock shriveled up and melted. They all recoiled.

"You die."

"Okay, so we're not spelling someone named Tom's name," Grog said. "Now what?"

"The message usually spells out something we just encountered," Eioffrey said. "So it's probably 'Gelatinous Cube.' "

"Great!" Ivan said.

"There's only one problem," Eioffrey said, a worried expression growing on his face. "I don't know how to spell 'Gelatinous.' "

Grog and Ivan stared at Eioffrey.

"I-it's okay!" Eioffrey stuttered. "It probably starts with a J."

He grabbed another stalagmite and poked a picture of a Jester. J. The stalagmite whipped away from Eioffrey's grasp and sprang upward, leaving behind nothing but a small crater that went up and out of the cave.

"Okay, it's G" Ivan said.

He poked a tile with a picture of a Gelatinous Cube with his foot. "Duh," he said as the tile lit up blue.

"Okay, that's great, but the door's not going to hold up too long," Grog said, the door behind them already disintegrating slowly, as if it were being eaten. Ivan stepped on a tile with a picture of a tiny Cupid on it. Grog and Eioffrey followed his footsteps.

"Eros. 'E.'"

"Light. 'L.'"

"Axe. 'A.'"

"Titan. 'T.'"

"Iris. 'I.'"

"Necromancer. 'N.'"

"Orc. 'O.'"

"Uranium. 'U.'"

"Silver. 'S.'"

Just as Ivan stepped on the tile *S,* the door flew open, falling on a dozen tiles and activating a million traps, destroying it. The mutation of Gelatinous Cubes flooded into the room, sliding over the tiles, picking them up and ripping them out of the ground, exposing the mechanisms beneath them.

Just as quickly as the entrance door flew open, the exit slid open, and Eioffrey, Ivan, and Grog ran outward.

The Gelatinous Mass roared angrily, like a mixture of a wild boar and a dragon with sinus congestion, and advanced, squeezing out of the same door the trio had entered from.

As they ran down the endless passages, Ivan turned to Eioffrey. "You're the smart one!" he yelled. "How can we defeat that thing?"

"Well," Eioffrey said, "There are ten kinds of 'bosses'. There are Duos, Trios, Work-alones, Maniacs, Kingers…."

"I'm not asking for a brief history on baddies!" Ivan yelled. "How can we defeat *that* thing?" he pointed backwards at the advancing Gelatinous Mass.

"Well, that would be classified as a Hulker," Eioffrey explained. "They usually have very low IQ and attack without strategy. They usually have a weak spot in a certain place that one wouldn't think."

"And where, pray tell, would that be?" Grog said.

"Since it's pretty dang stupid, it's weak spot would probably be where its brain would be," Eioffrey replied.

"But do Gelatinous Masses even have brains?" Grog asked.

"Of course!" Eioffrey said. "How would it have been able to follow us? Normal Gelatinous Cubes can't think because they have only enough cells to keep it alive. But when they join together, the brains also do, and it becomes conscious enough to feel and act, creating a Gelatinous Mass."

Ivan skidded to a stop and faced the Gelatinous Mass, drawing his sword. "That's all I need to know."

He leaped up above the Gelatinous Mass as Eioffrey protested, still charging, and sank his sword into the beast. The Gelatinous Mass let out an ear-spitting shriek before splitting into two smaller Gelatinous Masses.

Ivan growled, but before he could attack, he looked at his sword, Tri-blade. It had touched the Gelatinous Mass which was disintegrating right before his eyes.

"No!" he yelled, swiping at the sword as the top completely evaporated.

One of the Gelatinous Masses let out a noise he thought was supposed to be some kind of deep, echoing laughter, then reached out to evaporate Ivan, while the other turned to Eioffrey and Grog.

Ivan felt dumbstruck. Without his sword, he felt powerless. Every task he had completed, he only accomplished with his sword. He felt as if it was part of his own being. He relied on it a bit too much, and that had led it to him losing it.

Eioffrey and Grog looked at Ivan, then moved their attention to the Gelatinous Mass. Eioffrey summoned a magical blade, and Grog looked around before pulling out his frying pan from his waist belt and unconvincingly brandishing it like it was some kind of weapon.

It was the last thing Ivan saw before he blacked out.

"Wake up!" a voice yelled, then a force the size of a frying pan smacking his face.

"OW!" Ivan yelled, waking up.

Grog and Eioffrey stood above him, Grog was holding his frying pan in hand. He *had* smacked him in the face. Eioffrey had a stunned look on his face, then glared at Grog.

Grog hid the frying pan behind his back and started whistling unconvincingly.

Ivan rubbed his head. "What happened?" he asked.

Eioffrey swiped the frying pan from Grog's hand before turning back to Ivan and helping him up.

"You blacked out," he said. "And we defeated the Masses by ourselves. No thanks to *you*."

Eioffrey glared at Ivan, who was still waking up. His eyes wandered around until he spotted the hilt of his sword, the top gone.

"My-my *SWORD*!" he yelled.

He rushed up and grabbed what was left of it. Eioffrey, still glaring, walked over to him. "Come on," he said. "Get up. We need to keep moving."

Ivan turned and looked at Eioffrey. "You aren't in charge of me," he muttered. "You're just a kid. I'm staying here."

Eioffrey stared at him. "You're saying that like your sword was my fault."

"It is!" Ivan yelled. "If you had told me the Gelatinous Mass...."

"I *did* tell you!" Eioffrey yelled back. "Gelatinous Masses *and* Gelatinous Cubes have the same kind of melting power! It was your own mistake!"

"Oh, *really*?" Ivan shot back. "If we had followed your advice and stepped on that *J* tile, we all would have died, thanks to you!"

"It's not my fault I can't spell in English! I can only write and read in Halfling!"

While Ivan and Eioffrey argued, Grog wandered over to the remaining Gelatinous bits.

He looked back. "Guys?" he called over to them.

"What!?" Ivan and Eioffrey yelled in unison, turning in his direction.

"I-I think this might be edible."

Eioffrey groaned. "You say that about everything!"

"And it's true! And even I'm edible! But that is called cannibalism, my dear friends."

Ivan got up. "I don't need your guy's help," he said quietly. "I'm going to complete this quest by myself."

Eioffrey and Grog turned to Ivan. "No way," Grog said. "We're coming with you."

But Ivan had already started walking away, down the dark caverns.

Ivan trudged through the caves, his boots soggy from countless tripping in puddles. He had substituted his sword with a stalagmite, but it was not exactly the best kind of weapon. It would easily break against any foe.

Ivan had been walking for about ten minutes, and a deep, sinking guilt had already swam through his insides like a parasite, hunting for a weak spot. It seemed as though the guilt had already struck, due to the fact that Ivan had left his friends because of his own loss.

He had realized that without Eioffrey's smarts, and Grog's jolliness to keep them cheerful, he suddenly felt powerless and alone.

He paused, and turned, dropping the stalagmite, and running off the way he came, to find his friends.

He arrived at the place he had first left them. He looked around and spotted an object on the ground, sparkling. He bent down and picked it up. It was Eioffrey's pendant.

Odd.

Eioffrey never left his pendant behind. He treasured it like a gift, for it was. But something else caught Ivan's eye.

Grog's equipment.

This wasn't good. Ivan knew that these things were as precious to Eioffrey and Grog as his sword was to him. He looked around the cave. There was no sign of them. He shook his head and turned to go down a tunnel, but a voice suddenly rang through his ears.

"Ivan."

Ivan looked around. There was no one there.

"Ivan."

He turned again. He knew he wasn't imagining things, because what he saw assured him of that.

There was a hooded stranger, atop a column, with rock spires sprouting from the ceiling gripping Eioffrey and Grog.

Ivan's instincts kicked in before his train of thought did. He charged at the figure. The hooded person simply summoned another spire of rock and swatted Ivan like a fly, knocking him to the ground. Ivan found himself on the floor, coughing up dust when the figure came up to him.

"Hello," he simply said. His voice was as cold as ice.

Ivan didn't know who this person was, but all he knew was that he meant harm to him and his friends. And Ivan would not allow it.

"You're a bit reckless, aren't you?" he asked. He laughed, a sharp, painful laugh.

Ivan swiveled upward into a standing position and thrusted his fist into the stranger's face, knocking him into a wall. Ivan had relied on his sword so much that his fist felt as if it would break. As the figure emerged from the dust, Eioffrey yelled from his spire.

"Stop! Both of you!"

Ivan and the figure both looked up at him.

Eioffrey addressed the figure.

"Look, we don't want any trouble. We just need to finish our assignment and then we'll leave."

The stranger smiled.

"Well, as it would have it, *I* put up that notice. I've been watching you all for months."

"That's pretty creepy," Grog said, before a spire reached out and shut his mouth.

"You, Ivan, have been acting ridiculous. You put your sword before your friends, your family. Your own needs before the safety of others."

Ivan charged at the figure again. The figure caught his punch and threw him to the back of the dim cave.

The stranger walked up to him. "I cannot allow such negligence to thrive."

He raised his hand, causing small pillars to sprout from the ground and almost cover Ivan completely.

Ivan struggled against the Roc's holding him. Wasn't he strong enough? Why wasn't he able to break free?

"Tell me. Why should I let you live?" the figure asked.

Ivan struggled. He knew that if he didn't do something, he would die.

No.

His friends would die. His friends who helped him through countless battles and hardships. Friends that were there for him no matter what. Not just friends.

Family.

Slowly, his hands clenched into fists and tore the rocks off of his arms, sending them showering all over the ground. The figure's eyes widened as Ivan pulled the rest of his body forward.

"Because."

The figure backed away slowly. Ivan stared at him in the eyes, cracking his knuckles.

"Because they're my family."

He raised his fist and pummeled it toward the figure, sending him through countless walls, knocking him to the ground.

The spires fell apart, leaving Eioffrey and Grog falling towards the ground. Ivan ran, getting there just in time to catch them both.

Before any of them could say anything, the figure weakly stumbled back into the room. Ivan gently put his friends down and ran over to the figure, yanking off his hood. The man had a sharp, deadly looking moustache. His hair was curled in a way that might indicate that he was a wealthy person, as if he spent a lot of money on hair curlers. Ivan had given him a cut on the cheek.

"I obviously underestimated you, Ivan," he wheezed. "I'll be back."

Then he faded away with a snap of his fingers.

Five days later, Ivan and his friends sat at their table, drinking silently. They all were recovering from the event five days ago. Ivan was the first to talk.

"You guys."

Eioffrey and Grog turned to him.

"I-I understand if you don't want to be friends anymore. I was so self-absorbed with my own needs that I forgot about yours."

23

Eioffrey and Grog looked at each other. Then they turned back to Ivan, smiling.

"We forgive you," Grog said.

"And I'm sorry that I was so rude," Eioffrey said.

Ivan smiled at them. "Thank you," he said quietly.

"In fact, we have something for you," Grog said. "We saw it lying around in the cave."

Grog unzipped his bag and pulled out Ivan's sword. The exact same one. Ivan's eyes teared up as he reached over and sheathed the sword.

"After all," Eioffrey said.

Ivan looked up at them. His friends. His kind.

"We're family."

The Brothers

      The sun shone down on Guidway city, bringing a warm feeling to all who inhabited it. The flowers of Mrs. Weller's tiny garden outside her window bathed in the sunlight and flourished as they had never. The tall, towering hill of the guideway guild which usually cast a gloomy shadow, now welcomed all who looked at it with open arms. When Eioffrey strode out of his door, he looked around himself and had a wonderful feeling and confidence that today was going to be a wonderful day.

      Of course, he was wrong.

He started the day by complimenting Ms. Weller on her exquisite flower bed and engaging her in a friendly conversation, and then heading off to where he always went at 8:00 a.m. Nightshade Inn. Though the name was dark and brooding, today it sent off a jolly feeling. He opened the door with such confidence that Drugle, one of the ugliest townsfolk, gave him a toothy grin. Eioffrey sat down at his usual table with his friends Grog and Ivan. Grog was an Orc, and his hobby was cooking. Unlike the rest of his tribe, he viewed the pleasant side of everything. Ivan was a human like him, and, as Eioffrey thought, was a bit vain. He thought that Ivan was a bit presumptuous and headstrong, but admired him anyway, for his undying strength. They had saved him a chair as usual and already ordered him his juice. Though he was treated as an adult back at his home because he was rather big compared to the halflings, everyone here knew he was actually a kid, though he had the stomach of an adult.

"Lovely day, isn't it?" Grog inquired.

"Yes," Eioffrey replied. "Ms. Weller's flowers look exquisite, don't you think?"

Ivan laughed from his side of the table. "You two sound like old ladies, talking about gardening," he chuckled.

Old Flo rose from her seat across the room. Old Flo was, well, old. She hated "whippersnappers" and "punks."

"Hey, I take offense to that!" she shouted, picking up the first thing she saw and threw it at Ivan.

Fortunately, it was a newspaper, and it simply bounced off him. In a huff, Old Flo returned to her seat.

"I'm surprised that she heard that!" Eioffrey wondered quietly.

"I heard that too!" she yelled back.

Ivan sighed, picking the newspaper up from the ground and examining it. As Eioffrey sipped his juice, Ivan grew a shocked expression on his face. Eioffrey Looked up at him.

"What's wrong?" he asked.

Ivan laid the newspaper across the table. The headlining title was:

"NEW HEROES IN GUIDWAY"

And below it, the subtitle:

"QUARTZ SWORD STILL MISSING"

Grog leaned across the table. "That's us, right?" he said. Then, putting his fingers to his beard, said "But we didn't steal any sword."

"Apparently not," Ivan replied. "It says here that a group of 'Heroes…' " he raised his hands and did the quotation mark sign, "…saved a dwarf farmer named Jerome from a falling boulder, a few miles down."

"I know I don't know anybody named Jerome," Grog said.

"Anyway, after that, many people have been asking them for quests and stuff. They're calling themselves the 'Heroes of the Century.' That's all anyone knows about them."

He did the finger thing again and rolled his eyes.

"Speaking of quests, do we have any?" Eioffrey asked.

Ivan looked over to the Quest Board for the first time that day. It was completely vacant.

"I guess not," Grog sighed.

"I'm sure we can find some jobs if we look for them," Eioffrey said, patting Grog on the back.

Unfortunately, no one had any quests for them. The only 'quests' that anybody had were watering Ms. Weller's flowers while she ran errands, which Eioffrey obliged to, and washing Drugle's pantaloons.

After that chilling experience, the trio decided that they had enough of quests for that day. They decided instead, since these new heroes were rivals, to spy on them and find out how they did what they did. At first, they planned to hide where a disaster just might occur. But after two uneventful weeks, they pretty much gave up, until out came a newspaper with headlining title "NEW HEROES TO MAKE APPEARANCE TODAY." They packed all necessary needs and rushed off to the town square.

At first there was such a crowd that none of them could actually see the figures standing on the balcony, but as they got closer, they spotted them.

There was a half-reptile, half-human creature with eyes like a snake's, green speckled skin, and an oily tail that flicked back and forth.

Behind him, there was an Ogre that had a scar over one eye that seemed permanently shut, and a thick wooden club. Atop his head was a tiny top hat that curled around the edges. It looked ridiculous.

But in front of them both was a short person with a violent beard and a coat of an owlbear. He was too small to be a human, and too big to be an Imp. But Eioffrey recognized him without needing to see the coat, or the beard.

It was his brother.

Now, it wasn't his actual brother. It was his adoptive brother. When Eioffrey had been taken in by the halflings, Barvey was only two, and a rivalry quickly grew between them. Barvey knew all of his flaws and secrets and only kept them to himself for a reason Eioffrey never knew. But when Eioffrey spotted him, he seemed to turn to stone in place. Ivan spat on the ground, then turned to see Eioffrey as white as a ghost. After all, he hadn't seen Barvey after he disappeared several years ago. At the time, Eioffrey was eight. But seeing him now, it was like waking up to a different face. Soon, Barvey cleared his throat, and the crowd silenced.

"Good people of Guidway!" he said.

The crowd gazed intently at him.

"I would like to humbly thank you for taking time away from your daily schedule to meet us here! The Heroes of the Century!"

The crowd cheered, and Ivan spat on the ground again.

"Bosh," he muttered.

Someone in the crowd called "Thank you so much! We love you!"

Barvey grinned. "No, thank YOU! I'm so glad we could help! I can't even remember how much we've done for you!"

The reptilian creature pulled a piece of paper out of his pocket and unfolded it.

"Twenty-three questsssss, fifteen errandssss, piessss eaten: thirteen," he hissed. "And that wasss mossssstly Oble."

Barvey laughed nervously. "You've been keeping track?"

"You inssssstructed me to."

Barvey glared at the reptile. The snake man quickly folded the paper back into his pocket and kept quiet.

How would three people who obviously worked poorly together succeed in so many quests? Not to mention, eating thirteen pies, Eioffrey wondered.

"Anyways," Barvey resumed. "I have something to tell you all! I know that with everyone giving us all the quests, everyone else must be bored out of their minds!"

"Yes we are," Grog mumbled.

"So I would like to hold a contest! Whoever wins gets to take the whole week's quests! Because they must be much better heroes than us!"

The Ogre spoke up for the first time.

"Huh!' he warbled. "Heroes!" Barvey's smile cracked, but he somehow managed to regrow it.

Eioffrey suddenly felt a hand on his shoulder, and he turned around. It was Ivan.

"Come on," he muttered, glaring at Barvey and his crew. "Let's get out of here."

The challenge was all anyone was talking about in town. Only a few people actually joined, as the Guild had few employees, many only beginners. Everyone else in Guidway just wanted to watch. They were like moths around a lantern. Always liked good betting. Eioffrey had no interest in that. After all, he was just a kid. Since the trio had left early, they had missed the rules. Thankfully, somebody had posted them over the Quest board. Though Eioffrey didn't care about the contest, Ivan was throwing an eternal fit.

"They can't just decide who gets quests!" he shouted. "That's the guildmaster's job! They're not even part of the guild!"

He picked up a random potion off the table where they were studying them and threw it on the ground. The glass shattered and a cloud shaped like a Turkey leg emerged from the wreckage.

Eioffrey stared at the image before it disappeared. Then he turned to Ivan.

"Well, there's only one thing we can do to get our jobs back," he said. "Win the contest."

The next day, Ivan, Grog, and Eioffrey signed up for the contest, though Ivan gave the attendant the stink eye the whole time. As Eioffrey peeked at the list, he sighed. There were only four contestant teams, including them, and they all were all from the guild. After that, Ivan seemed to cheer up to the days leading up to the contest. On the day of the contest, all the competitors were summoned to the town square along with the rest of the village as well. There was a giant stage in the middle along with hundreds of chairs surrounding it. Once everyone had arrived, a goblin walked up onto the stage and reread the rules.

He cleared his throat. "Good people of Guidway," he coughed. He was old. "I am honored to present to you the most excitement we've had since that walrus juggled a few bananas a few months ago."

Eioffrey remembered the walrus. It was silly.

"But now we have excitement that is even greater!" he wheezed. "We have a challe-" his speech was interrupted by a sore throat. He flipped open a pocket and dropped a few pills into his mouth as the audience blankly stared at him.

He quickly resumed. "A challenge!" he said, more vigorously.

The crowd cheered.

"The rules are simple, he continued. "We will have two teams fight against each other in different types of contests, battling in the forms of Swordsmanship, Magic, and Revivement! But since we don't have any conveniently injured people, it will be a cooking contest."

After the brief speech, the four teams stepped out of the crowd. Eioffrey had had no time the previous day to see exactly which teams had signed up. But now he got a pretty good look. One of the first teams was not a very experienced one, as they were beginners. The name was Team Tanzanite and it consisted of a female elf, a dwarf, and a human. They would be easy to beat, for none of them had experience in Revivement. Revivment was the act or job of healing, like a carry-on doctor. Next was a more intimidating team, Team Ruby. Three Orcs, all of them brutal and reckless. Their names were Jon, Jorah, and Francis. They were all brothers, and equally bloodthirsty. They would be hard to beat in combat. Finally there was one of the most elite teams in the guild Team Zircon, consisting of a Human named Calepryen, an elf named Soravv, and a Half-Breed named Torundous. Since they had experience in all fields, they would be hard to beat. The Old goblin called attention again.

"Two groups of two teams will face one another. The groups that win will then fight each other. Then the group who wins that will challenge the Heroes of the century! If they win, they get first dibs on quests! If, not, the Heroes of the Century will get first dibs as before,"

"Heroes of the Century," Ivan scoffed.

The four teams were split up. Thankfully, the trio was set with Team Tanzanite, the inexperienced team. There had been a bit of a delay at first, with the other team needing to figure out which one of them would take part in Revivement. After that had been figured out, Ivan and the dwarf stepped up and unsheathed their swords. The goblin told them they had to knock the opponent off the ring to win. Once they started, the fight was fierce. Ivan would jab, then the dwarf. Finally, Ivan and the dwarf clashed swords, and Ivan pushed him back. As the dwarf landed outside the ring, a loud bell rang. The crowd cheered, and the dwarf stepped back up to scowl at Ivan. Next, Eioffrey and the elf were up for Magic. They would try their best to wow the crowd. They stepped up, and the elf winked at him. He blushed. He was a stranger to flirting, but then realized elves were usually far older than they looked. This one was probably at least fifty, though she looked like she was something like fourteen. The goblin announced that the contestants needed to put on a performance and wow the crowd best they could. The elf stepped up, releasing a shower of fireworks. The crowd oohed. Eioffrey stepped up, shooting out a handful of Pink glowing flowers that exploded into a shower of millions of tiny petals that covered the audience. They cheered. The elf scowled, releasing at least twenty dragon-like shapes that twirled around, then joined together and exploded into an enormous dragon face. She turned to him.

"Let's see if you can do better," she whispered.

Eioffrey clamped his hands together, pulling out a seed. The elf stifled a snort. But just then, Eioffrey threw it in the air. It landed, causing a ripple effect. Suddenly, a tree sprouted from the place where the seed landed. The tree then grew hundreds of small bubbles that floated down the crowd. Some of them

32

reached up and tried to pop them. As soon as the tree evaporated, the crowd cheered wildly. Eioffrey took a bow. The elf just crossed her arms and sulked off the stage. Eioffrey was feeling confident.   Maybe they really could win this!

The human that was chosen to take place in Revivement was pretty terrible at it. Apparently he had joined the team because of the elf's flirtation.

Guess he doesn't know how old elves are, Eioffrey thought.

While Grog made a delectable stew out of cabbage and dandelions, the human made a mess in his cauldron. Lizards legs, weeds, and random bits of meat floated around in his. The judges reluctantly handed Grog the badge without even needing to taste the human's concoction.

When they began round two, Team Zircon had beaten team Ruby. Though team Chaneseek was more experienced, Eioffrey, Ivan, and Grog had more inventory. It was close, but the trio won. It had been boring at first, but now, knowing they were almost there, made them more confident.

Ivan was up first. He was to face the reptilian man, whose name was Iris. Iris was a swordsman.

Or is it Swordsnake? Eioffrey thought. It puzzled him.

When Iris and Ivan entered the ring, Iris' tongue flicked in and out. They drew their swords and started fencing. Iris had a technique unlike any Eioffrey had seen. And by the looks of it, Ivan had never seen it either. Iris would strike, then jump back, preventing Ivan from getting a good shot at him. They continued this way for a while. Eioffrey noted that Iris stopped flicking his tongue. He wondered why, because snakes used their tongues for smelling. Eioffrey thought it would have helped Iris, but he seemed to be fine, dodging Ivan's blows.

The crowd started to get bored. A couple of people yawned and looked up at the sky. Suddenly, Eioffrey heard a noise. He turned to the ring, and saw Ivan blocking his eyes. Iris lunged at him, kicking him in the gut and sending him flying out of the ring. The crowd cheered as Eioffrey and Grog ran over to Ivan. As they helped him up, Ivan opened his mouth.

"He cheated," Ivan said.

Eioffrey was stunned. "How?"

Ivan got up shakily. "He flicked his tongue at the start. He was playing with me, moving me around. I was looking at him, and he flicked his tongue. There was some kind of light that blinded me. Next thing I know, I'm coughing up dust."

Eioffrey turned to Iris, who was slithering down the steps of the ring wearing a look of self-satisfaction.

"Ivan said you cheated," Eioffrey said.

"Ludicrousssss," Iris hissed. "How could I have cheated?"

Eioffrey stammered. He didn't know exactly how Iris could have cheated. Iris leaned down and flicked his tongue. A wide grin appeared on his face.

"Sssssssee?" he whispered. He smiled an unnerving smile and walked off, his tail slithering behind him.

Next was Revivment. Grog lined up with the Ogre, whose name was Oble. Oble's tiny hat was perched atop his head, threatening to fall at the slightest movement. Oble peeked at Grog with a discolored eye, making him flinch. Once it started, Oble and Grog started selecting certain items and dropping them into their cauldrons. But when Eioffrey looked closely, he saw that Oble would look at Grog's choice, then drop the same thing into his bowl, mixing it up a few times with other ingredients. Eioffrey tried to tell the judges, but he couldn't reach them.

When the judges clambered up the steps, Eioffrey drew in a breath as they reached Oble's cauldron. They reached in a ladle and took a sip. The judge rose, made a face, and moved onto Grog's. Eioffrey glanced at his brother who was glaring at

Oble. The judges tasted Grog's, and smiled, handing him a badge. They had won.

Eioffrey sat on his stool, thinking to himself. As far as he knew, Barvey had never practiced any magic. He didn't even have a pendant. He was wondering how he planned to win, but knowing Barvey, he probably had a nasty trick up his five-inch sleeve. As he stepped up onto the stage, he and his brother stood across from one another.

Barvey smirked.

That was bad.

"Well," Barvey said, breaking the silence. "Hello, Eioffrey. Brother."

The crowd started whispering.

"Yes, this is true. Eioffrey is my brother. From Patapata Town." He faced Eioffrey. "And he was the reason I left."

The crowd gasped. Clearly they disapproved of Eioffrey 'exiling' their 'savior.'

"Ever since, I've been wandering around. My only goal is to become a legend. And that meant becoming a hero. Our father chose you over me, just because you could use magic and I couldn't."

He turned back to the crowd.

"It is also true that I have no experience in magic. But who needs magic, when this *fool* is using it so badly."

He jabbed a finger at Eioffrey. Eioffrey's brain started whirling, trying to figure out what he meant by that.

"I mean, look at him!" he continued. "Look at his hair!"

The crowd obliged.

"How do you think it got blue?"

Eioffrey covered his hair. He spotted Ivan and Grog looking at him curiously.

At the Halfling Village, Eioffrey had been conducting an experiment with the elder, Panch. During the experiment, an enormous explosion had left his hair swirling and blue.

And now Barvey was retelling the whole story to the crowd, who were laughing all the while.

"My haaaaaair, my haaaaaaaiir!" Barvey yelled, doing an impression of Eioffrey. The crowd guffawed.

"Who do you want to be your hero?" Barvey asked the crowd.

"You! You! You!" the call rang out, getting louder.

"BARVEY! BARVEY! BARVEY!"

Eioffrey covered his ears to block out the horrid sound piercing his ears

"BARVEY! BARVEY! BAR...."

Suddenly, a giant rumble shook the ground and ceased the chanting. Everyone turned to where the source had come from, and found themselves looking at the mountain of Guidway Guild.

As the rumbling stopped, the stairs lining up to the top slid into the mountain, and a hole appeared in the bottom. A mist poured out from the hole as a figure rose from.

The Guildmaster sure knew how to make an entrance.

Eioffrey had only met the Guildmaster a few times. Ivan, Grog, and him were applying for the Guild, and he gave them the position after a while. But now, watching him in all his glory, staring back at the crowd, a shiver ran down his spine. The Guildmaster approached Barvey and threw back his hood.

"What is this!" Barvey yelled. "Get off my stage, old man!"

The crowd drew in a quick breath. Barvey looked around in confusion just as the Guildmaster swiftly kicked Barvey's leg from the back, pushed him into a leaning position, and threw Barvey's sword on the ground.

The Quartz sword. The one that had been missing for months.

The crowd gasped. Barvey's face went a shade of flustered red. He desperately reached out to sheathe the sword, but the Guild master kicked it away. For a man in his fifties, he definitely was agile.

"Get off me, you fool!" Barvey yelled with a hint of terror in his tone. "Don't you know who I am?!"

The Guildmaster glared at Barvey like an eagle looking at a mouse it had been trying to catch.

"Don't you know who *I* am?" the Guildmaster hissed.

Barvey blinked.

"I run the guild. You have taken ownership of its rules when you were not allowed to. I was only alerted of it just now."

He turned to the crowd, casting a hateful shadow.

"And only Old Flo thought to tell me."

Old Flo stood up from the crowd.

"Hah! Payback!"

The Guildmaster turned back to Barvey.

"The officers will be very happy to get their hands on the thief of the Quartz sword."

The contest had crashed, and it was over. Barvey and his lackeys had been taken into custody. New rules had been appointed for the Guild, and from then on the Guildmaster would be a part of as much as he could. Old Flo received a reward, and now lived in a cottage at the top of a hill. Eioffrey's life had pretty much gone back to normal, but people would sometimes look at his hair.

A few days later, Eioffrey was in his cottage, which he shared with Grog and Ivan. Well, more like they shared it with him. It was pretty small. Flowers used to be on the window, but they died out quickly. They were replaced by a cactus. A portrait of a rather ugly woman that Ivan called 'Grammy' hung on the wall next to Grog's cooking equipment. Eioffrey had plenty of possessions when he left Patapata town to venture the world, but most of it was either stolen, used, or lost. His pendant was fortunate enough to escape that demise. Eioffrey's boots, soggy and muddy trudged on the welcome mat and he threw them in the pile of various unmatched shoes of different style and color. He sat down on the sofa they had found abandoned under rubble a few years ago. It let out a defiant moan as dust flew out from the bottom. He sat, looking at the clock's finger tick by before a knock at the door came.

Eioffrey sat up quickly. They almost never had visitors, and the mail goblin always left the stuff there. Eioffrey held his pendant steady and approached the door.

It was an officer.

Eioffrey blinked. This was the same kind of officer that held Barvey's arrest. The officer broke the silence.

"Someone wants to see you," he said, in a dry tone. "Before he leaves for jail for the next ten years."

Eioffrey knew who it was even before he stepped into the light.

Barvey.

"I want to apologize," Barvey said, hanging his head. "From the bottom of my heart."

Eioffrey stepped back.

"*What* heart?" Eioffrey asked. "Seems to me like you don't have one to apologize from. You lied to everyone. I didn't banish you. You disappeared."

Barvey took a deep breath.

"You did. Before you came, I was in the spotlight. Everyone adored me. Father was proud, mother said I was a prince. Then, you came. Discarded by the wretched humans you thought to be your parents. They were no parents. They left you all alone, a baby, in the Roaming Woods to be fed upon. When father brought you in, all the other Halflings turned their focus on you. I was no longer a star, a prince that father and mother

38

cherished. They were always like: 'Be nice to your brother' and 'you're too old for that'. So one day, I left. I felt as if I had no more meaning there. I stumbled upon those two idiots," he said, jabbing his finger at Oble and Iris. "Ever since, I've been trying to become a star again. Seems I've taken the wrong path, though."

He sighed, looking down at his feet. Eioffrey looked at him. They stayed like that for a long time.

"Finish up!" one of the guards said, tapping on the window.

Eioffrey turned to the window, then back to Barvey.

He walked forward, and hugged him.

Barvey stiffened up, but paused, and embraced him.

They stood there for a minute. The guards eventually came back in, and took Barvey back.

"Eioffrey?" Barvey said.

Eioffrey turned his head.

"I love you."

Eioffrey smiled.

"I love you too."

The Circus

Vanilla looked out the window of her compartment on the train. She was an acrobat, part of the Emerald Circus. The train raced along the tracks, passing the Oyster Ocean. In the front of the train, her brother Manti was shovelling coal into the flames that powered the train. He was a genius, and never let anyone forget. The train itself was built and painted by Aro, her sister. Aro might be just ten, but she was even smarter than Manti, and she knew it.

The train of Emerald Circus was delicately painted with precise details of talents and feats, each one expressed as its own story. Vanilla was the athletic one (more or less) and found joy in dangerous things. Naturally, she was the trapeze artist because of her flexibility and talent. They all were part of the circus, which travelled all over the land. Even though her life was an amazing one, there was still something missing.

Grog woke up on the floor, like usual. His blankets were five feet away from him. Eioffrey was on his back, still snoring. Eioffrey was only eleven, but *man*, did he snore. Grog gently picked up Eioffrey and laid him back on the bed. Grog tiptoed down the small hallway and peeked into Ivan's room. Ivan was sitting up, rubbing his eyes and picking his teeth. Grog wandered into the small kitchen. It wasn't much, but he loved it. He was a fantastic chef and had both an enormous repertoire and sense of taste. He only felt as if one thing was missing in his life, but he couldn't quite put his finger on it.

Ivan wandered out into the kitchen where Grog was now making eggs.

"Hey, Ivan!" Grog called over to the 22-year old man bumping into furniture as he tried to find a chair.

Ivan mumbled a greeting.

"Want your eggs scrambled?" Grog ventured, hoping to get a single word out of Ivan.

"Sure," Ivan mumbled as he reached out to find his boots.

Grog cracked five eggs for Ivan and began scrambling them. Eioffrey now came out of his and Grog's room, brushing his hair and with his shirt on inside out *and* backwards.

"Eioffrey," Grog whispered.

Eioffrey sleepily looked up at Grog, brushing his swirling blue hair.

"Your shirt."

Eioffrey looked down, snapped his fingers, and his shirt warped into the right way it was supposed to be.

Unfortunately, that caused his hair to tangle again. Eioffrey grumbled and went back to brushing his hair.

Grog spotted Ivan searching for the newspaper. Grog picked it up from the counter and tossed it to him. Ivan's quick reflexes caught it in mid-air, bringing it down and opening it, falling on the couch.

Five weeks ago, Eioffrey's brother had pretty much taken over the Guild that Grog, Eioffrey, and Ivan were a part of. They had won, but Eioffrey's brother had been banished from the town. And ever since then, Eioffrey was extremely sensitive about how his hair looked.

Ivan had been a nervous wreck because he had actually been beaten in a match of swordsmanship. His opponent, Iris, cheated, but he still sulked nevertheless. Grog seemed to be the less fazed, probably because he was the only one that had beaten his opponent. Grog was a deluxe chef, after all.

But because Eioffrey and Ivan were moping around, Grog wanted to do something fun for them. He didn't quite know what, though. Eioffrey and Ivan didn't share much interests.

He peered over at Ivan, who apparently found nothing interesting in the newspaper. Grog picked it up. Ivan never read the front page, well, not after the challenge of the Guild. Grog immediately saw what was on the front page:

"CIRCUS VISITING, COME SEE AMAZING FEATS!"

Grog had found the day's entertainment.

When Grog had told Eioffrey and Ivan about their trip to the circus that day, they were thrilled. If there was one thing they had in common, it was a love of entertainment. They headed out the door and down the street. The circus tent was miles away, but they could still see the colorful top with a flag waving gracefully in the wind. Once they got there, it was already 6:27 p.m. The circus would open in three minutes. As the trio approached the tent, which was more beautiful than it was from afar, it took them a minute to realize that the ushers were mimes. Not the fun, silly kind of mimes, but the creepy, unsettling kind. They wore black jumpsuits with hard, white masks that had an emotionless and blank stare. As Eioffrey, Ivan and Grog passed them and handed them their tickets, the one on the left seemed to be watching Eioffrey closely. Eioffrey shuddered and clung onto Grog's arm. Once they had passed, Grog got Eioffrey some popcorn. That cooled him down a bit. The circus began at 6:30 sharp, and it began with a bang. Once the smoke cleared, a tall man in a top hat with a sharp mustache emerged from the dust.

He introduced himself as Vance, the Ringmaster. He discussed the history of the circus to the crowd, who sat amazed the whole time, save Ivan. He peered at the man, like he had seen him before. Grog had fallen asleep by the time he was done. Eioffrey woke him up twenty minutes later, when the clowns were on. Grog himself had no interest in this circus, but he enjoyed it for Eioffrey and Ivan's sake.

Slowly Grog started nodding off while the clowns continued drawing laughter from the audience. He slept peacefully until he was awakened by a voice over a loudspeaker saying:

"And now, Vanilla, the trapeze artist!"

Grog woke up, looking around. His eyes slowly followed the beams of light up, where an elegant figure was poised atop a single ledge.

And as the lights shone on her, Grog felt his heart melt. She was simply beautiful. He watched her every movement as she swung from beam to beam, twirling in the air ever so often. Grog sat there, entranced, watching her long robes follow her like thousands of bright, glittering reflections. Even after she had finished, he paid no attention to any of the other acts. He only thought of Vanilla and her beauty. He started to doze off in happiness.

"Grog...," a voice faintly called. Grog awoke, sleepily looking at Eioffrey and Ivan who were looming over him. Eioffrey staring intensely into his eyes.

"Sorry, that must've been really boring for you," Ivan said apologetically. "Ready to go home?"

Grog nodded, getting up and lumbering out the tent. On the walk home, Ivan and Eioffrey discussed their favorite acts with each other. When Eioffrey asked what Grog's was, he just shrugged. That night though, all Grog thought about was Vanilla. He lay awake, wondering when he could see her again. Eventually, he drifted to sleep, but not after many hours of thinking.

The next morning, Grog was flipping pancakes when Eioffrey walked up to him and asked:

"Can we go back?"

Grog nearly dropped all the pancakes he was juggling on the frying pan. Once he caught them, he turned to Eioffrey.

"Well, I think we need to ask Ivan what he thinks."

"IVANNNN!!!!!" Eioffrey hollered. Ivan stumbled out of his room, pulling his boots up and with his shirt half-on.

"What?" Ivan yelled back.

"DO YOU WANT TO GO BACK TO THE CIRCUS?!?!"

"Sure, but is it okay with you?" he asked Grog. Grog shrugged.

After Eioffrey and Grog finished scarfing down their pancakes, they made their way back to the circus, which was already crowded with people. Grog managed to shove his way through, trying to avoid eye contact with the Mimes, who still stared at Eioffrey. Grog kept his hands on Eioffrey's shoulders, guiding him into the tent. They sat down, and this time Grog kept his eyes wide open to look for Vanilla. Eventually she came, and bowed as the crowd cheered wildly. She swung from bar to bar, but Grog could tell there was something wrong. She seemed less focused than before. She moved with less confidence, and Grog hung on the edge of his seat.

Suddenly, as Vanilla reached out for her next bar, her hand slipped and the world plunged into slow motion. Grog leaped out of his seat and dashed toward Vanilla as she fell. Everyone else in the tent seemed frozen in time as Grog jumped onto the stage and caught Vanilla. Once she stopped blinking in confusion, she turned her head towards him, and for a fleeting second, they stared at each other. Her beautiful sparkling eyes gazing at his loving brown ones. The time after that was a blur. Stagehands came on, escorting Grog away from her, as they led her offstage. The stagehands led Grog outside the tent, setting him on a bench. The show continued, but Grog was too lost in a daze to watch.

When the show was over, everyone flooded out of the tent, peering nervously at Grog, who still sat at the bench. Eioffrey and Ivan approached him, Eioffrey trying to read him.

"You can go home," Grog said. "I need to think."

Eioffrey hesitated, then hugged him. Ivan waved a good-bye, and they left. Grog sat there, and soon enough a worker found him.

"Hey, you!" he yelled. "What do you think you're doing here? The circus is closed for the night!"

Grog stammered. "U-uh, sorry."

Suddenly, a calm voice called out.

"Don't worry, Saliem. He's with me."

Vanilla stepped out into the light.

Saliem choked. "S-sorry, Miss Aura," he apologized. "I-I didn't know."

"It's alright, Saliem," she said. "Don't you have business over at Manti's cabin?"

"Y-yes," he stammered. "I shall take my leave."

Saliem scooted away. Once she was sure Saliem was gone, Vanilla turned to Grog. His heart skipped a beat.

"I never got the chance to thank you earlier," she said. "Mind if I sit down?"

"S-sure," Grog said, scooting over. She sat next to him.

"You know, you and Saliem seem alike," she said. "I think you'd like him once you get to know him. I did."

There was an awkward pause.

"You're pretty amazing," Grog said. "You're really good at acrobatics."

"Thank you," Vanilla said, blushing.

"Literally, I was asleep for most of the time," Grog said, laughing. "I kinda just came here for my friends, but you were amazing. Really."

"Oh, the small one with blue hair and the edgy guy?"

Grog chuckled. "Yep, that's them. Eioffrey and Ivan."

There was a silence again.

"Um," Vanilla said. "We're kinda taking a break from performing tomorrow."

Grog blinked. "Oh! Is it because of your fall? I'm really sorry."

"Um, actually," she said, blushing harder, "I was wondering if you were free. I'd like to get to know you."

Now Grog was the one blushing. Was she really asking him out? What were the odds?

"Um, yeah," he said.

"G-great," she replied. "Moonset Hills? At 12:30? Want to go there?"

"Sure."

She got up and waved him goodbye. He waved back. As she disappeared into the darkness, Grog got up, with a happy feeling in his bones, and left for home.

Grog slept so well that night that Eioffrey had to pull on his long, greasy black hair, waking him up quite rudely. Grog sprung up and almost slapped Eioffrey across the room before he realized it was him.

"S-sorry," Grog apologized.

"Jeez, those hands flip pancakes!" Ivan chuckled.

Grog sat up and rubbed his eyes. He looked at Eioffrey, who was glaring at him.

"You're supposed to make breakfast!" he said in frustration. "And It's Twelve-o-clock!"

Grog's eyes widened. "Twelve?!" he jumped up. Twelve-thirty was when he had his date to meet Vanilla! Grog dashed to his drawer, and put on the nicest shirt he could find. As he ran out the door, he yelled:

"Sorry, guys! I've got... something to do! I'll see you later!"

As he left, Ivan turned to Eioffrey.

They looked at each other.

"Know how to cook?" Ivan asked.

For the first date of his life, it had gone pretty well. He had met up with Vanilla at moonset hills, and had a wonderful time eating macarons and talking about their daily lives. Vanilla told Grog that she and her siblings were part of this travelling circus, and Grog told her about his life living with Ivan and Eioffrey. They spent countless hours like this until they realized they were so caught up in talking that they didn't notice the sun setting over the horizon. They said goodbye, and went home. When Grog opened his door, Ivan was waiting for him.

"Well," Ivan said, lounging on the couch. "Long 'thing' you had to do."

"Sorry," Grog apologized. "I lost track of time. Where's Eioffrey?"

"We went to the circus, but those two freaks with masks didn't let us in. Said they were closed for the day. Eioffrey got upset looking at them, so we left. He's in your guys' room."

"Thanks," Grog said. He kicked off his boots into a pile of dozens of footwear and made his way to the bedroom. When he went in, Eioffrey was huddled up, swathered in blankets. He clutched his pendant.

"Hey, Eiof," Grog said. Eioffrey didn't respond.

As Grog sat next to him, Eioffrey mumbled, "It's Vance."

"What?" Grog asked.

Eioffrey turned towards him in a daze. "Huh? Oh, hi, Grog,"

"Who's Vance?" Grog asked.

"Who?"

"Vance. You just said: 'It's Vance'. What do you mean?" Eioffrey stared at him in confusion.

"I-I didn't say anything...."

When Vanilla climbed into her cabin, she set her basket down and pulled off her slippers. She untied her hair, and slowly, she sat on her sofa, letting out a sigh. A few seconds later, the door slammed open. Manti burst in, clearly out of breath. Running was not his strong suit. His Eye-scope was still attached to his head, and his sleeveless jacket was wrinkled.

"Hello, Manti," Vanilla sighed.

Manti seemed to forget what he was doing for a minute. Then he regained his balance, and stood up.

"V-Vance needs to see you," he said, still gasping. "Something important."

"Vance? The Ringmaster? Why would he want to see me?"

"I dunno!" Manti said. "He never tells me anything!"

Vanilla got up. "Well, I'll go over to his cabin. Then I am coming back to sleep. So do not interrupt my slumber."

Manti shuffled his way out of the cabin. Vanilla followed, eventually making her way to Vance's cabin. His was painted red with speckles of white, including designs of magic. She had never seen Vance do any magic, but it seemed to be a kind of a heritage.

As she approached the cabin, she saw the two mimes standing guard. Those two had always freaked Vanilla out, with their emotionless masks and bony figures. She constantly wondered why Vance kept them around. When she came closer, the mimes parted and opened the door to the cabin. When she entered, Vance was at his desk, his feet propped up on the mantle.

"Vanilla! Welcome!" he said, getting up and putting his arm around her, leading her to an empty chair as he motioned for the mimes to close and lock the door.

"How are you doing? I heard the fall was dramatic!" he said, laughing. His moustache seemed to threaten her.

Vanilla let out a nervous chuckle. "Y-yeah. Dramatic."

He sat back down and looked at her. There was a silence that followed. He stared intently into her eyes, and then blinked.

"How have your 'dates' been?" he asked.

Vanilla choked. How did he know?

"You probably don't know everything about me," Vance said. His gaze was unsettling, like a predator watching its prey.

"You two seem close," he continued, getting up and pacing around her. "And his friend..."

"I-Ivan?" Vanilla stuttered.

Vance considered this. "No," he said, shaking his head. "The...the small one."

"Eioffrey? What about him?" Vanilla said, turning her head to look at Vance. The scar on his cheek seemed to pulse with anger.

"Yes... that's him. His pendant is curious."

"W-what do you want with it?"

Vance laughed. A cold, evil laugh. He paced around, casting his long dark shadow around her.

"It has the power I need. With that power, I may finally avenge my father's death. I may punish the people who were responsible."

Vanilla had never known something had happened to his father, he never said anything of the sort. Well, not until now. He turned back to her. Smiling a wide, broken smile.

"Halflings," he said, clenching his fists. "They were responsible. Sure, maybe he cheated at a few games of poker, got a few of them drunk and made them do stupid things. But them killing him was unacceptable. They must be punished for their treachery. And as they always say, fight fire with fire."

Vanilla looked at him cautiously. "So...what do you want me to do?"

"Bring the boy to me. And if you fail...."

He pulled out something that looked like a syringe out of his desk. The thing was filled with glowing black liquid that pulsed around and emitted a dark energy.

"Well, let's just hope it doesn't come to that."

As the next few days passed by, Grog noticed that Vanilla became quieter whenever the subject of his friends would come up, and her eyes would wander, trying to change the subject. But one day Grog just couldn't take it anymore.

"Vanilla," he said. She looked at him, flinching.

"Are you all right?"

She blinked. "O-of c-course!" she stuttered.

"Are you sure?" he inquired, leaning closer. "You've been acting kind of strange for the past few days. Is there anything I can do?"

"N-no!" she said. "I'm fine."

She reached out and took another muffin coated in chocolate chips, biting a chunk out. Grog reached out too, but not to take a muffin, but her hand.

"Hey," he said, looking into her eyes. "You know I'm here for you, right? That you can tell me anything?"

She didn't reply. Grog sat back, gazing into the red leaves in the tree above them. A long silence followed, until Vanilla put down her muffin and looked at Grog with a worried expression in her face.

"Grog," she said.

"What?"

She looked around, as if to make sure they were alone.

"I need to tell you something."

Grog sped down the path to his home. Vanilla had told him that Vance, the Ringmaster of the circus, was planning to capture Eioffrey and use his magic. He was running so fast, that he tripped and fell on the ground. When he got up, his nose was bleeding. He rubbed it off and kept running. He eventually made his way to the cottage on the hill. Grog gasped. The door had been kicked down off its hinges. He ran in and saw that most of the furniture had been turned over or ripped to shreds. He spotted Ivan laying in a heap on the ground with a black eye and slimy things that looked like seaweed encasing him. Grog leapt over the broken remains of objects and ripped the vines off of Ivan. He coughed, looking at Grog.

"Vance. He was the one who led us astray in the mission to Bludmud cave... they took Eioffrey," he said. "I don't know why. So... fast."

Ivan promptly fainted.

Grog set Ivan down on a more comfortable spot of broken furniture and ran out to find the circus. He eventually got there, but the door was suspiciously left open.

"It's a trap," Grog said to himself. "Fifty Parvs say so."

He walked in. In front of him was a blank stage, empty seats. No traps activated.

"Huh," Grog said. "I guess...."

Suddenly, a giant cage fell from the ceiling, trapping Grog. He sighed, as a spotlight fell on him. He looked up, covering his eyes.

"Well, well, well!" a voice called. A figure fell from the ceiling on a giant chain. "Did you really think you'd make it this far?"

"Actually," Grog said. "I was expecting a trap."

The figure leapt down. "Shut up! It took me long enough to build this thing on such short notice!" He stepped into the light. It was Vance.

"You're the one who attacked us in Bludmud cave! You're the one who almost killed us!" Grog exclaimed.

"Yes," Vance said. "It might have been a hassle putting that mic onto Vanilla to see what she said, but in the end it was worth it. Not like she knew! After all, now I have you in a cage, Vanilla tied up, and your little friend who's about to be drained of his magic!" he laughed maniacally. Grog sighed. He had been in a situation like this exact one before. They had been fighting pirates.

"Watch him," Vance said to an unseen person. "And if he tries to escape, you have my permission to do whatever you want. I am NOT having another hero ruin my plans,"

As Vance walked off, two figures approached the cage. Grog recognized them. The Mimes. Their cold, hard stares kept him in place. He had been thinking of chewing off the bars as he had once, but the mimes wouldn't take their eyes off of him.

Eventually Grog gave up trying to stare out the mimes. He just sort of curled up and laid down on the cold floor. After what he thought half an hour had passed, he had given up. Eioffrey was probably dead, and the world was doomed. He glared at the mimes, who stared blankly at him. Suddenly, a blade sprouted from one of the mime's faces, cracking the mask and squirting black goop all around. The mime fell down, and on top of it was Ivan, sticking his sword into its back.

"Ivan!" Grog yelled. But Ivan couldn't talk, as he parried a blow from the furious second mime.

"Get out of the cage and rescue Eloffrey!" Ivan yelled back to him. "I'll deal with these guys!"

Grog nodded and got to work chewing up the bars. He ripped them off with his teeth and ran out of the cage, towards the way Vance had gone. He entered a room with candles in various places and saw Eioffrey chained up on a wall with markings on it. Vance stood in front of him with his back showing to Grog, but he turned around immediately.

"What!" he exclaimed. "How- never mind! You're too late to stop me now!" he pulled out a bottle and spilled the contents underneath Eioffrey.

"Zhunderhcak, oujiviok, gerusti..." he started to chant, but Grog interrupted him with a frying pan to the head, making him crumple to the floor. Grog ran over to Eioffrey, who was unconscious. He slapped him gently, waking him up. He ripped off the chains, and he pulled Eioffrey off the altar just as it lit up in blue flames. Ivan ran in, with a mime mask kebab in his hands. Eioffrey hugged them both, and Vance struggled to get up.

"I..." he started, coughing out blood. "I will return...."

He dragged himself over to the flames and leapt inside them. He disappeared, his form flickering.

The next day, Eioffrey was in the hospital while the circus packed up. Grog had gone to see Vanilla. He had to ask her something. He ran into her as he turned the corner, and he screeched to a stop.

"Oh!" Vanilla exclaimed. "Hello, Grog."

"Hey, Vanilla," he said.

They looked at each other in silence.

"How have... how have you been?" he asked eventually.

"Good," was all she said. He noticed a bag trailing behind her.

"Where are you going?" he asked.

She sighed. "The Emerald Circus has kind of fallen apart since Vance basically tried to destroy this place," she said. "Without a leader, they don't have anywhere to go. So I decided to take charge and lead them myself."

"But that means..." Grog realized what it meant before she said it.

"I need to leave. I may come back, I may not."

Grog nodded. How could fate be so cruel, to tempt him with the love of his life, only to send her away?

"Well, I guess...."

Suddenly, Vanilla leapt forward and kissed him. His mind went blank. It had happened so quickly. He stood there, while Vanilla blushed and ran off to the tents that were packing up. He watched her, her elegant form sparkling in reality. He felt lucky, to have for once, experienced love. He looked at the swirling leaves above him and embraced himself.

The Beginning

As Ivan dashed down the hallways of the crumbling castle, he panted, trying to get away as fast as possible from the ravaging storm behind him. He could waste no time looking behind, seeing his memories ripped from him and swallowed by the darkness that would eventually consume all. He had grown up here and couldn't bear to see it torn away. He eventually made it to the long and spacious bridge that connected the castle to the fertile ground. He knew he should've kept running, but he needed to see his home one more time. He turned around just as a gargantuan black being shot out of the highest tower. It roared in victory, spreading an aura of dark matter all around the land, causing every plant to wilt in submission. More spires of dark, writhing matter shot out of the castle, destroying it with an ear-splitting scream. It was then that Ivan chose to run, vowing never to die as all his family had.

Eioffrey had woken up to his adoptive mother's calm whispering.

"Eioffrey..," she said, stroking his blue hair. "Time to get up. Your father wants to see you."

He sat up slowly, rubbing his eyes. His mother was exactly his own height, because she was a halfling, and he was a human. In fact, every person in the village was a halfling except him. He had been raised by them, for his own parents had abandoned him and left him in the woods. He got out of bed and walked over to the drawer, putting on a shirt and the pendant his father gave him. He slipped on his sandals and walked out of the cottage, crossing over the thousands of branches that served as pathways for the halfling village. He eventually made his way to his adoptive father's house, inside of the giant tree that connected the town. The old wood door hung firmly on its steel hinges, refusing to break off no matter how hard the force. As Eioffrey opened it, he spotted his adoptive father rummaging through some drawers. Eloffrey approached him cautiously, trying not to scare him. But it didn't matter because his father turned around so fast he scared the living daylights out of both of them.

"Eioffrey!" the old man cried. "You can't do stuff like that!"

Eioffrey got back up. "Sorry, I didn't mean to," he said.

The old man smiled. "Well, at least you aren't as threatening as your brother. He scares me all the time."

Eioffrey laughed. His brother Barvey was kind of a jerk to everyone in town for reasons unknown. He constantly enjoyed scaring people or disturbing them.

His father got up.

"Eioffrey," he said. "I need to tell you something."

He led Eioffrey further down into the tree, underneath roots and passing tiny homes of critters made inside the tree. Eventually his father led him to a heavy metal door with markings engraved on it. His father turned to him.

"Can you move this, Eioffrey?" he asked.

Eioffrey looked at the door. There were no locks, only the door itself. It probably weighed over five hundred pounds. Eioffrey readied his pendant. He shot out a beam of light which grabbed the door and slowly pulled it open. His father then led him inside. He opened a vault, and pulled out a crystal, turning to Eioffrey.

"Eloffrey," he said. "This is a spirit-summoning crystal. I believe you are more than mature enough to use it."

Eioffery marvelled at the intricate designs on the crystal, how it sparkled in the dim light, emitting a bright, spiritual energy. He looked up at his father who had a sad look on his face.

"You need to share this wonderful magic you possess with the rest of the world," he said. "This spirit crystal will protect you as long as your pendant lies on your neck." He wiped a tear from his cheek and placed the crystal into the pendant, making it glow bright blue. He looked up at Eioffrey.

Eioffrey hugged his father. "I love you, Dad."

His father hugged him back. "I love you too. Now go, make me proud."

"Grog!" Bloodstain yelled. "Get your lazy butt out here!"

Grog, the 14-year-old Orc, stumbled out of his bedroom with his pajamas still on. He ran into a stack of axes, knocking them over and spilling them all over the floor. Bloodstain groaned, marching over to the mess, picking up the lot and tossing them to the side.

"Come on, you waste of space," Bloodstain snarled. "Let's make you useful."

He led Grog out of the house, dragging him by his wrist, and brought him to the training grounds where the rest of the Orc men fought to prepare for war. But Grog didn't like violence and only wanted to use it as a last resort. He much more enjoyed cooking. The scent that filled the air when you added a touch of lavender to the chicken stew, the satisfying *splump* that occurred when you sprinkled the blackberries inside the pie.

"Grog!" Bloodstain yelled, pulling his long, delicate black hair. "Wakey-wakey!"

He handed Grog an axe and ordered him to start hacking at a steel post, as if it were an enemy. Grog reluctantly trudged forward and gave a weak swing at the post. The axe promptly got stuck. Grog tried pulling on it, but his arms weren't made for heavy lifting, but for precise handiwork, and he couldn't pull it out.

Bloodstain growled, stomping over to Grog and yanked out the ax.

"This," he said, swinging the axe at an alarming speed, cutting it into two, "is how it's done."

He walked back to Grog, handing him the ax.

"And if you don't improve," he whispered, "you're next."

'ALL PASSENGERS BOARDING FOR REVERB PORT, PLEASE HEAD OVER TO AIRCRAFT 12!' a voice on a loudspeaker called. Ivan dashed to the crowd gathering at the loudspeaker's request and tried blending in with them. He, along with the other passengers, moved along until they came to the docks where the majestic airship lay. He occasionally bumped into other passengers as they growled things like "watch it," or "Look where you're goin, pipsqueak." When they got to the gate, a pilot stood guard and took tickets. Ivan didn't have one, so he tried hiding. But his attempts were futile.

"Hey!" the pilot called. "Kid! What're you doing? Where's your ticket?"

Ivan stopped in his tracks. He looked over to the pilot. Sure enough, the pilot was looking in his direction.

"I said, where's your ticket?" People were starting to look in his way.

"I-I," Ivan stuttered. He wanted everyone to look away and go on about their own business. Their gaze pressed down on him like

"If you don't give me a ticket, you're not..."

Suddenly a man in a dark cape and wide-brimmed hat walked up and put his hand on Ivan's shoulder.

"Not to worry, he's with me," the man said, in a smooth, silky voice. He held out two tickets for the pilot to see. "I'm just taking him over to Guidway City for a visit."

The pilot inspected the tickets, then grunted. He took them and stamped them both with a red marker. He gestured for them to board the ship.

"Make sure to stay with me," the man said to Ivan before they went aboard. Ivan just looked up at him warily. They boarded the ship and sat down on two seats next to each other.

The man in the cape made sure the pilot was out of earshot before he turned to Ivan.

"That was a close call," he said, taking off his hat, revealing sharp, black hair. "You need to work on your stealth."

Ivan just looked at the man.

The man looked back. "I'm Fryor," he said, holding out his hand. Ivan reached out his, shaking Fryor's.

"Ivan," Ivan said.

"You seem a bit young to be traveling on your own," Fryor said. "How old are you?"

"N-Nine," Ivan said.

Fryor studied him. Ivan didn't like being studied.

"You seem of royal descent, one way or another," Fryor finally said. "What're your parents? Squires?"

"Dead."

Eioffrey had spent less than a week traveling by himself, and he was still terrified of all the new and different things surrounding him. He had never been outside of Patapata town, and all the un-magical, sometimes lifeless things scared him. He hadn't even met anyone, which scared him even more. The map his father gave him was an outdated one, and several things on it were either not there or in rubble. He decided to head to the Roaming Woods and seek refuge there. Roaming Woods was an eerie, silent forest that seemed to cast a deep, smothering night over itself. The twisted trees looked as if they were alive, but few signs of life were perceivable. Eioffrey did his best to break up firewood with his small hands and eventually made a campfire, taking in the lessons from his father. The forest was cold, but the heat from the fire was warm enough to give comfort. Eioffrey sat down and held up his pendant, gazing into the beautiful patterns and colors it emitted. This, at least, let him know he was not alone in this forest.

Suddenly, a distant *CRASH* shook the forest. Eioffrey got up. What if it was a monster? A demon?

But it was neither of those things. A large, circular shape seemed to have descended from the sky.

A blimp. Eloffrey thought, *These are what father told me transports people around the world.*

But this blimp wasn't a friendly one, full of happy tourists. Eioffrey could hear the voices coming closer, some of them yelling jovially, others in commanding tones. Finally, a loud voice cut through the others, sending them silent.

"All right," the voice said. "I want all of you to spread out and start looking. If Rilo's right, then we'll have some magic."

The other people cheered.

They're talking about me, Eioffrey thought. *They must be talking about me.*

He quickly took a bottle of water and spilled the contents over the fire. It disappeared, but the sudden disappearance of light caught the people's attention. The cheers stopped as quickly as the fire had. Eioffrey muttered one of the few halfling curses that existed and started running. He quickly regretted that too, because the leaves underneath his feet made deafening crunches that undoubtedly alerted the people where he was going. They started running after him, yelling for him to stop. But Eioffrey refused to stop running. Eventually he made his way into a dark clearing. He bent down to catch his breath, then kept running. But he hadn't even taken a first step when his foot swung up, caught in a net. He dangled there for a second and eventually the people caught up. One came close, raised a club and knocked Eioffrey out.

When Grog finally returned home, he was exhausted. His father had forced him through several hours of endless training, techniques and constant slaps on the head for not paying attention and watching the butterflies. He fell face first onto what he thought was his soft bed, but instead fell on a hard slab of rock, almost breaking his face. He yelped in pain and got up. His mother Camile instantly ran in at the sound of his shriek.

"Grog!"she yelled. "Are you okay?"

Grog looked at her, his pupils readjusting themselves. "Why is there a stone slab where my bed is supposed to be?"

His mother looked ashamed. "Your father wanted to 'toughen' you up. I didn't know this was what he had in mind." She looked at the slab.

"Not even the same size," she muttered. She turned back to him.

"Well, want to help me make dinner?"

Grog's face lit up. "Yes!"

He followed her into the kitchen where a comforting aroma beckoned him. Above the fireplace hung a cauldron where the scent emitted.

"Soup?" he asked.

"Soup."

Grog eagerly rushed over to the table, picking up various ingredients. He set them down and laid them out, pulling out a cutting knife and chopping them up into tiny bits. His mother watched, gazing at him lovingly as he threw them into the cauldron. Eventually Grog dipped in a ladle and took a sip of the soup. His face lit up cheerily, and he turned to see his mother's expression. But when he faced her, he saw his father, Bloodstain, staring at him with a mixture of bewilderment and anger.

Ivan and Fryor sat on a wall, staring into the harbor of Reverb Port. It was a calm place. They watched the crimson sun set over the horizon. Fryor had brought him there to talk, but they just sat in silence.

"How?" he eventually asked, cutting the silence.

Ivan turned to him. It had been a while since he had thought of what had happened, but the thought of it gave him goosebumps.

"I-I don't want to talk about it," he said in a quiet tone.

Fryor just looked at him. "So then how did you survive the wastelands?"

The wastelands were what now disconnected the rest of the Northern Continent from the Kingdom Axlea, his homeland.

"Hitchhiking."

Fryor nodded. "And how did you protect yourself?"

"I didn't," Ivan said, lifting up his sleeve and revealing a deep scar on his left arm.

Fryor nodded again, getting up. He held out his hand for Ivan.

"Where are we going?" Ivan asked.

"We're gonna make you a sword."

Fryor led Ivan to a cave a distance away from the harbor. Inside lay a menagerie of tongs, hammers, and chisels. There was a cauldron that looked full of a boiling liquid, emitting an intense heat. Hanging on the walls were dozens of swords of all shapes and sizes. Fryor gestured to a solid steel table, with various molds in the shapes of swords. They spent the next hour making the perfect mold for Ivan, measuring the width, and what weight he could carry. Then they poured the boiling metal into the mold, watching it seep in. Ivan and Fryor then decided to take a rest from the heat and went outside while the metal cooled down. But when they came back, the liquid metal had seeped onto the edges, leaving a jagged, rough looking sword.

"You may want to make another one," Fryor suggested, but Ivan shook his head.

"This is perfect,"

He raised the blade in the air, the blade shimmering in the hot red light.

Eioffrey woke up chained up to a beam, his wrists bound tightly, and his leg attached to a heavy ball with an iron chain. He looked around, seeing he was in a room with no one else in it. Two people guarded the door. He quickly noticed his pendant was still on him, thankfully. He realized why soon.

"I can't believe Prymar wants to keep the pendant with him," one of the guards said.

'You know Prymar," said the other. "He doesn't think too much of children. And neither should we."

"I know, but..," the first voice said, "couldn't he just escape?"

The other one laughed. "He is but a *child*. He can't use that hunk of junk, even if he tried."

The guards fell silent. After about thirty minutes, someone else came to the door. One of the guards seemed to have a negative reaction to this.

"Hey," he said. "What are you doing? Who authorized you to do this?"

The new person, a tiny man, responded: "Prymar wants us to feed him to make him more 'Suggestible.' Make him think we're on his side."

The guard sighed. "Fine. Make it quick. He's asleep anyways."

The door slipped open, and the new man stepped in. Eioffrey quickly hung his head to make it look as if he was still asleep. The man set down the tray of food and looked at Eioffrey, making sure he was asleep. Then he slowly tiptoed up to him and reached out to touch his pendant. It was now that Eioffrey decided to attack. He quickly swung his fist, knocking the man out cold. He took the keys hanging from the man's waist and unlocked his wrists and foot. He immediately took the man's cape off and put it on himself, pulling the hood far over his head. He then placed the man where he had been and locked him into place, and walked out, trying to avoid the guards who waved him a goodbye, thinking he was the other man. He simply waved back and started navigating the hallways of the blimp. It was lit by dim lights that decorated the walls. He quickly realized that this wasn't just a ship, but a pirate ship. He searched for an exit, but to no avail. He just wandered down the endless hallways until he ran into another pirate.

"Hey watch where you're going, Rilo..." he began, but then saw Eloffrey's face. The man's own face went pale as he quickly pulled out a large horn and blew on it, sounding the alarm. Soon, others went off in various areas around the whole ship until the whole place was filled with the sound. The pirate reached out to grab him, but Eioffrey swiftly kicked the man in the face, not knocking him out, but stunning him momentarily.

"Sorry," Eioffrey said, taking off. "You were trying to capture me."

Eioffrey leaped over the man, who lay on the ground now. Eioffrey kept running, eventually finding a large expanse, the back of the ship, with a large opening at the very end. He started towards it, but he heard a *bang* and found himself in a net. He fell to the ground, and a dozen voices cheered. Eioffrey tried looking at them and saw a big, burly man with an eyepatch and a mechanical leg. Atop his square head he wore a long black hat.

He bent down to look Eloffrey in the eyes. "Ye' think ye' could escape my ship?" he smiled a long, grimacing smile. "Well, Ye' were wrong." He turned to the other pirates. "Let's get this over with."

He reached out for Eioffrey's pendant, his eyes transfixed with its beauty and promise of power. But at the last second, a giant beam of blue light shot out of it, filling up the whole ship, and it formed a long, graceful being. The spirit looked down at the pirates, using a simple swipe of its hand to knock them all away, piling them into a stack. It then turned to the captain, sucking in some air and releasing it on him, having him join the stack too. It finally turned to the heavy metal door and ripped it in two. Eioffrey jumped, bringing the spirit with him. He fell, not realizing they were already in the air and landed in a thick tree. He brushed the leaves off his face and drowsily looked up at the ship which was starting to fly off-course, Eioffrey decided then to head to Guidway city, where he could be safe.

Grog sat in the chair, strapped there by the murderous gaze of his father. Bloodstain had been furious when he saw Grog cooking. It wasn't the fact that he was doing it, it was because he was actually *enjoying* it. In Bloodstain's point of view, he had been raising Grog for the sole purpose of holding up his name, no other reason. Grog neglected battle training and instead chose to take his mother's path. So naturally, Bloodstain was enraged.

"You've got a lot of nerve," he said, intensifying his glare on Grog.

"You're taking this a bit too seriously," his mother said, gently laying her hand on Bloodstain's. He shrugged it off, glaring at her.

"This doesn't concern you," he shouted. "Go back to cooking."

Camile flushed bright red, let out a deep breath, and obeyed him. Bloodstain turned back to Grog.

"You're a Bullhorn," he continued. Bullhorn was their last name. "Our line has been fighting wars for centuries, and for you to choose cooking over our past." He shook his head. "You've taken this too far."

Grog looked over at his mother, who was glaring at his father. He had never seen her do that before. Bloodstain continued.

"I refuse to have a child who does not follow me," he said. "You are to leave the premises and never come back."

Grog was shocked. He hadn't expected his father to do this, but then again, his father *was* Bloodstain. He had a vicious reputation amongst all Orcs, even their majesties. He intimidated all, sending all he glared at into a state of fear. But he could tell his father was not kidding the slightest bit. Grog started to tear up.

"You have one hour to pack your things and leave. Maybe being on your own will toughen you up a little."

Grog slumped in his room. He packed his favorite clothes, his frying pan, and several mood rings his mom had gotten him. They usually emitted a plain, blue happiness, but now was an eerie mix of white and brown. This was an unusual pattern that had never appeared before. As he walked towards the door, his Mom gave him a hug that squeezed nearly all the air out of him.

"I want you to know two things," she said. "I will always love you, no matter who you are or what you become. And if I could, I would stop this from ever happening."

She kissed him on the cheek. He hugged her tightly, until he saw Bloodstain glaring at him, and he left then. He walked to the large walls that surrounded Orkro Kingdom and took one glance at his home. It might've been his last, even. So he savored it, burning the image into his head. He turned around and set off for a new home.

Chapter 1

Nightshade Inn was not a very pleasant place that night. A fight had broken out between a goblin and a dwarf about who could withstand the most horrible monsters, and they started fighting each other, punching the other in the face repeatedly, knocking glasses over each other's heads, and basically destroying everything that came in their path. Ivan didn't care as long as they didn't interrupt him polishing his sword. But it was inevitable, and soon the dwarf shoved the goblin into Ivan.

"Watch it," Ivan growled. He might've been puny as a nine-year old, but the twenty-one year old man was much more than intimidating, and his blade was as sharp as his wit. The goblin and dwarf immediately backed off. Ivan turned back to his sword after making sure they would stay out of the way. Ivan decided it would be best to leave and quickly swallowed his beer. He slapped some Parvs on the table as payment, a common kind of silver. He strapped his sword onto his shoulder and left Nightshade Inn. He strode down the cobblestone pathway, following it to the Guidway Guild, the official 'Police for Hire' in the Southern Continent. He walked up the twisting stone stair up to the very top of the mountain. The structure of the Guidway Guild was a very creative one. It started at the top with a simple dome. But inside, it led to an underground facility where requests were taken and given to various members of the Guild. Some of the

Guild members who had no homes to call their own slept there, but thankfully Fryor had let Ivan live with him. And that was where Ivan was headed. The shack was well kept, even though it was decades old. Ivan knocked on the door, and a faint voice called out.

"Come in."

Ivan opened the door fully. Inside he saw Fryor who was now fifty-seven years old, laying on the soft sofa, and was mostly unable to move due to a sickness he had caught. Ivan strode up, pulling out a packet of food for Fryor. He opened it up, releasing the delicious smell of Steamed Beetroot stem and Fried Pork Balls with rice, Fryor's favorite dish. He smiled, taking the food. He reached out to give Ivan a hug. Ivan happily returned it.

"How are things at the Guild?" Fryor asked.

"Good enough," Ivan said. "Varnian and his team just came back from the Agate expedition in one piece."

Fryor laughed. "I never expected them to come out of that alive."

He took a fork and jabbed at the Pork Balls, sticking one in his mouth. He made a sound of delight.

"How are things here?" Ivan asked after Fryor was done chewing.

"Good enough," Fryor said. They both laughed. "Oh," he said, pulling out a letter. "This was for you. From the Guild."

Ivan took the envelope and tore it open. Inside it said this:

Dear Ivan Greyhem, Team Amber, Number 15.

Noting the retirement of your partner, Fryor Greyhem, we have come upon the opportunity to assign you new partners. We know you work alone, but these are new recruits, and they need a strong leader. We have chosen you. Please come to the Guild at 7:30 pm sharp.

Yours, the Guidway Guild

Ivan growled in dismissal. He threw the letter on the ground.

"They expect me to replace these people with you?" he said, turning to Fryor.

Fryor took a spoonful of rice and swallowed it. "Ivan," he said, "the Guild needs you to help lead these people. And I think both you and I know I'm not coming back to the Guild."

Ivan grunted, stepping outside and checking the position of the sun. Exactly 7:00. Ivan sighed, walking back into the shack.

"I guess I'll need to go soon," he said. Fryor smiled. He knew Ivan meant now.

As Ivan walked out the door, heading for Guidway Guild, Ivan tried picturing what the new teammates might look like. He hated to admit it, but he was excited to finally have some teammates for the first time in forever. He thought of an elf, an Ogre, maybe even a Halfling. He would be really lucky if he got a Halfling, they were master magic users. He spent the rest of the time walking to the Guild wondering about his new teammates, what their skills would be, and what they might look like. But what he expected was not even close to reality.

Chapter 2

Eioffrey had to be honest. He hated Guidway City. He had to make money to feed himself by performing magic tricks to civilians, and some of the time they didn't even pay attention, like they'd seen better magic. Eioffrey was barely making it, anyway. He had gotten close to wanting to use his magic against those people, but his father had told him never to use his magic against others unless they were attacking you. Eioffrey hated that rule now. He had felt as if he wouldn't make it, until a lucky poster flew into his face. He pulled it off, attempting to crush it for daring to interrupt his sleep. But when he saw what it said, it completely changed his mind.

Recruits needed!

The local Guidway Guild has been running low on adventurers! We need you to join today! It requires a simple test in your chosen skill! Please report to the Guidway Guild from 7:20 am to 11:00 pm!

Join today!

Eioffrey's eyes widened. He got up immediately and climbed onto the roof of the nearest building, looking for the tall mountain on which Guidway Guild lay. He spotted it almost at once. He leapt off the roof and ran in its direction. It was raining hard. Eioffrey ran into several people on his way. He eventually made his way to the towering stairs that led up to the peak. He dashed up, skipping every other step until he came to the top.

Now, when Eioffrey had imagined the Guild, he was picturing a majestic palace full of warriors and magic. But what he actually saw was a simple dome, held up by simple wood.

Eioffrey cautiously approached the dome, looking at its every angle. The entrance was barred, and a small hole (small enough for only a small rabbit to fit through) poked out in front. But once he stepped on the hole, something shot up and hit his foot, sending it flying back up as a periscope took his foot's place. Eioffrey looked at it as a slit opened and an eye blinked, obviously looking at him.

"Who are you?" the thing shouted at him.

Eioffrey blinked. Was the periscope talking?

"I said, who are you?" it repeated. "What are you here for? I certainly know I haven't seen *you* before!" The eye seemed to be the thing controlling the periscope, like a brain controlling a body.

"Me? I-I came because of the...." Eioffrey said, pulling out the poster. The periscope inspected it.

"Mmmmmmmm... fine," it said. "Please proceed inside and stand on the platinum disc."

As Eioffrey wandered inside the dome, he heard the periscope mutter: "I swear, everyone always looks at me like I'm some sort of monster."

In the middle of the room, as the periscope predicted, was a platinum disc about the size of a circular bed. Of course, the only bed Eioffrey ever slept on was a halfling bed, so this disc was much larger than the bed he was used to. He stepped onto it, and for a second, nothing happened. But then suddenly platinum rods shot out of the bottom of the disc and attached themselves to Eioffrey's feet. Then, the disc shot down into the ground at 50 miles an hour. As it passed the earthy walls, Eioffrey was still recovering from the sudden drop. He felt as if he had left his stomach at the entrance. He eventually ended up at some sort of cavern. Eioffrey looked around and saw lamps hanging on the walls giving light. Inside the lamps were crystals emitting a neon green. It seemed to Eioffrey that he needed to pass down the cavern, so he did. It seemed to go down endlessly, until he was led into a wide expanse where structures of steel and dwellings were made. The dwellings were leveled differently, some on tall spires, others directly on the ground. On the left side was another tunnel with a sign that said *Dining Hall*, and a few more passages. At the end of the expanse was a giant doorway with two door knockers. Eioffrey could smell the scent of stew in the air. But instead of following the aroma, he walked over to someone who was clearly building one of the dwellings.

"Excuse me?" Eioffrey said. The person turned around and Eioffrey got a good look at them. He was a Dragonborn, a half dragon, half human creature. He had red scales that reached down to his upper chest before melting into the human tones. He had dragon feet and a tail. He wore a sharp vest and had cargo shorts.

"Yes?" he asked in a fiery tone.

"Where do I sign up for this?" Eioffrey held up the invitation for him to inspect. The dragonborn pointed to one of the tunnels.

"Go down there, then take a right. You can't miss it."

"Thanks," Eioffrey said, taking off down the tunnel, following his instructions. He soon met a door with a sign that said *Training Ground*. Eioffrey knocked, opening the door. Inside he saw various weapons hanging on walls, protruding out of dummies and in the hands of Sparrers. Above them all were people in robes taking notes. *Judges*, Eioffrey thought. He could spot another door at the end marked *Magic Users*. Eioffrey walked over there, opening the door. He had expected there to be more people, but there was no one there, except for a man in robes on a high deck similar to the one in the swordsmanship room. The man immediately spotted him.

"Excuse me," the man called down. "Are you here to sign up?"

"Yes!" Eioffrey said.

"Well," the man said. "You're the first one in two weeks. Let's see what you've got."

Chapter 3

Grog was sulking. He had found a job (thankfully), but he hated it. Sure, he could cook, but he never got paid enough to feed himself, for the restaurant was in the middle of nowhere, and he couldn't ever get enough ingredients. Besides, the manager was never nice to him, always criticizing him and his work. He constantly was having things shouted at him like "Grog, this stew is over*stew*ed!" or "You're using two day-old ingredients!" or even "Too much *Broth* in the *Broth*!" Basically, he was trying to ruin Grog's life. And since Grog never made enough money, he had to sleep in the storage room. There were rats in there too, and their squeaking kept him up all night.

"Grog!" his manager yelled. Grog blinked out of his daze.

"What?" he asked. "Let me guess, the patties are too *pattie*."

"No, one of our customers spilled his drink. Clean it up."

Grog peered over the counter. He saw a goblin had fallen asleep, knocking over his drink.

"I think he's our *only* customer."

"Whatever," his manager said. "Just clean it up. Then bill him."

Grog sighed, grabbing his mop and going over to the goblin to wipe up the mess. After he finished, he took out the bill for the goblin and gently laid it in front of him. This same goblin had been coming to Sal's Diner for the past week, and he had said he would pay them when he was completely finished. *Yeah right*, Grog thought. This goblin would never pay them.

"Grog!" his manager yelled again. Grog got up, realizing he was just standing there, looking through the window at the swirling purple clouds.

"Snap out of it! We've got more customers!"

Grog looked up and saw three figures at the door. An elf with half an ear, a dwarf with a violently long beard, and some kind of tall, pale creature with shadowy skin. They all sat down at a table, eyeing the goblin.

"Don't mind him," Grog said. "He's just had a bit too much to drink."

The dwarf grunted.

"What would you like?" Grog asked, handing them the menu.

The elf, dwarf, and thing looked at the menu.

"I'll take some waffles, thanks," the elf said.

"I'll have some steak, cooked crispy," said the dwarf.

Grog looked at the Thing expectantly. It didn't even move.

"Ah," the elf said. "Our dear friend here would like some leftovers. As rotten as possible, if you can."

Grog had plenty of rotting food. They didn't have a fridge, so they had to use up food quickly. Grog ran into the cellar and came back with a few tons of the stuff and set it down in front of the creature. It eagerly sucked it up like it was inhaling it. It afterwards licked the remains up with its long black tongue.

Grog noticed the trio spent the time eating and also looking at the goblin intensely. At one point, the elf took out a piece of paper and held it up, looking at it, and then looked at the goblin.

"Is something wrong?" he asked eventually. The elf looked at him, then put his hand up to whisper.

"Do you know who he is, exactly?" the elf asked in a quiet tone, pointing at the goblin.

"No," Grog said.

"He's an outlaw. He's stolen from some of the richest people in the Northern Continent. We're from the Guidway Guild, trying to find him and arrest him." The elf held up the wanted poster. Sure enough, this goblin was on it. His name was Indigo and underneath his picture were the words: *Reward if found: 50,000$* In Parvs.

Grog now looked at the goblin in a whole new way. Instead of a lazy and arrogant goblin, he saw a deadly and dangerous outlaw.

"We were hoping to just take him while he was asleep, if that's okay."

Grog was just fine with that, but he might've had a hard time explaining the situation to his manager.

"Let me tell my manager first," Grog said. He dashed into the cellar and explained the situation to his manager, who wanted to make sure. When they got back, the elf showed him the poster.

"I see," his manager said. "You can take him. But he owes us a lot, so we'd need part of the reward."

The elf sighed. "All right, fine. How much does he owe you?"

His manager turned to Grog expectantly.

"About 730$ in Pravs," Grog said, after calculating.

"Well, thank you," the elf said.

"You should probably get him soon," his manager said.

The dwarf nodded, and he and the elf lugged him out of there, the Thing trailing behind them. Grog turned to his manager.

"I was thinking," Grog said. "If you're getting paid all this, could I go?"

It was very sudden and straightforward, but his manager just said:

"Sure."

Grog practically leapt down into the cellar, grabbing his bags and cooking equipment (including his favorite frying pan) and skipped out the door as his manager stared at him with an uneasy gaze.

Since Grog just quit his job, he had to find a new one. And he knew exactly where….

Chapter 4

Ivan was walking to the Guild when he ran into a small man. Well, more like the man ran into him. He knocked them both over, and once Ivan got back up, he helped the tiny man who seemed to have trouble getting back up due to the ginormous backpack attached to his back.

"Are you alright?" Ivan asked.

The tiny man growled. "I'm *fine*. Get out of my way," he said, and promptly kept running without asking Ivan if *he* was okay.

Ivan looked as the man limped away. He seemed to have something heavy in his backpack, lugging him down.

At first Ivan wanted to go after him, but he needed to go to the Guild. So he went there, ignoring his instincts. He followed the path that eventually led to the Guild, walking up the many steps. When he got to the top, the periscope shot up and confronted him.

"Hello, Ivan," it said. "You were called for a meeting to meet your teammates. Please proceed to chamber 7."

"Nice to see you too, Peri," Ivan sighed. "Did you get a haircut?"

"Incorrect," Peri said. "I do not grow hair."

But Ivan had already gone ahead, ignoring the periscope. He shot down on the platinum disc, reaching the lower floor. He stepped out, following the lights into chamber 7, knocking on the door. He was greeted by Loram, the halfling who served as advisor to the Guildmaster. He seemed extra grumpy today.

"You're late," Loram growled.

"Maybe you're just early," Ivan shot back. "Where are they?"

Loram led him to a door and pulled out some keys. As he did so, Ivan was tingling with anticipation. But when he opened the door, Ivan saw an Orc sitting at a table stacking cards, assisted by a small kid with blue hair. When they saw Loram and Ivan, they both spun around in their chairs, knocking over the stack of cards. Loram slapped his head.

"I told you two not to touch those!" he yelled, rushing to gather them all. Ivan just stared at them. When Loram had finished, Ivan asked:

"Are these them?"

Loram let out a deep breath. "Yes."

Ivan looked at them.

"Could I talk to the Guildmaster?" Ivan asked.

He soon found himself in the Guildmaster's office. The walls were covered in banners. Several treasures laid across the desk. There was a giant fireplace at the back.

"What do you need, Ivan?" the Guildmaster asked in his usual smooth tone.

"It's about my new partners," Ivan said. "They seem...odd."

"Why so?" the Guildmaster asked, pulling out a branch from his drawer.

"I mean, one of them is a kid, and the other looks like an imbecile! There is absolutely no way these guys can replace Fryor."

The Guildmaster sighed. "Ivan, when you've been around as long as I have, you try to find the potential in everyone, even if they might not look like it. Why, the small one was the only magic-user who showed up, and he still got to the Gold Rank. And the Orc was better than anyone I've ever seen at cooking. His stew is delicious!" he laid his hand on Ivan's shoulder.

"Just give them a chance," he said.

Ivan sighed. "Okay."

The Guildmaster smiled. "Because every branch can blossom," he said, as the twig he was holding bloomed with beautiful red flowers.

Ivan was led back to the room where the two were waiting. Loram cleared his throat.

"Eioffrey, Grog, meet Ivan, your leader. He will...well...*lead* you in your quests."

There was an awkward silence as they looked at each other, then Ivan. He simply waved back.

"Are there any questions?" Loram asked. "Because I've got things to do."

The Orc raised his hand.

"Yes, Grog?" Loram said.

"I, um, don't have a house," he said nervously.

"Not to worry, you can take one of our dwellings to sleep in until you get a house for yourself," Loram said, pointing out the window to the tiny houses scattered across the Guild's spacious floor.

The child, Eioffrey, raised his hand. "Can I have one, too?" he asked.

"Yes, you may," Loram said, handing them both keys with the dwelling numbers on them. They both left, heading to the dwellings. Ivan looked as they passed, then got up, planning to head for home. But Loram stopped him.

"Ivan," he said.

"What, Loram?" Ivan sighed.

"I need you to make sure no one comes into chamber 13, ok? I'll pay you to stand guard. I'm having a meeting with some of the counselors."

Ivan looked at him with a mixture of confusion and pride. Loram never asked Ivan to do anything for him! And getting paid twice in one day was a pretty sweet deal, too. So Ivan followed Loram to chamber 13 and leaned against the door, casting a glare at anyone who looked like they might think of going in. Eventually the meeting ended, and Loram slipped Ivan a coin the size of his palm.

"What's this coin?" Ivan asked.

"A wandering coin," Loram whispered. "You can't really buy anything with it, but it's rare."

Ivan looked at the intricate designs on the coin. It showed a man with a stick, lugging a backpack behind him. But when Ivan looked up to ask Loram where he got it, he was gone.

Chapter 5

Eioffrey was actually starting to like the Guild, with all its beautiful lights illuminating the walls and the cozy feel of the dwelling he now lived in. He had already organized all of his possessions and other items around the space, and he had already made a friend, the Orc. He had expected him to be violent and dangerous, but he was actually pretty calm, and liked doing quiet activities. And he also now lived in the dwelling next to Eioffrey's! Eioffrey had just met his team leader, Ivan, who seemed kind of mysterious, though.

It was evening, and Eioffrey had been wondering when it would be time for dinner. He was starving, and the hours he had spent training tired him. He missed his father's Dandelion Salad. He was a vegetarian. He soon heard a bell ringing, and a loud voice calling "DINNER!" at the top of his lungs.

Eioffrey soon got to the tunnel with the sign saying **Dining Hall** along with the other Guild Members. As he sat down on the table he noticed quickly that there were at least 17 Guild members at the table, whereas yesterday there were at least 50. But his attention was soon brought to the front of the table, where there was a goblin who had a big pot in front of him. The Guild members started tingling in anticipation, as the goblin removed the lid and was assisted by a big, hunking troll to split the food among all the Guild members. But Eioffrey noticed that they were serving steak, which Eioffrey didn't like for two reasons. One was because he was a vegetarian, and two, because his teeth couldn't chew food that thick. So when they got to Eioffrey's plate, he declined any food, just resorting to the orange juice. But his stomach ached for some actual food, and the entire meal felt like torture. When it was finally over, Eioffrey was clinging to his stomach and headed over to his dwelling when he noticed the Orc lumbering over a small cauldron, cooking something that smelled delicious. As he got closer, he saw the Orc take out some leaves of lettuce and dip them in beans and sprinkle it with salt. The aroma beckoned Eioffrey, and he soon found himself sitting next to the Orc, who was looking at him uneasily. Eioffrey turned to him in surprise, not realizing he had just walked over there.

"S-sorry," Eioffrey said. "It just smelled so good."

"That's okay," the Orc said. "You want some?"

"Sure," Eioffrey said. "What is it?"

"I'm not sure what to call it," the Orc said. "I kind of just made it up."

"Wow," was all Eioffrey could say. He watched as the Orc gave him one, taking in the smell. The lettuce had hardened over the beans, making a sort of taco. Eioffrey took a bite, and his eyes lit up with joy. He ate it up, enjoying every bite until there was nothing left.

"Wow," said the Orc. " You eat fast!"

"Sorry," said Eioffrey. "I'm a vegetarian and steak was for dinner. So I didn't really get anything to eat."

"Yeah, I'm not really used to eating anyone else's cooking," the Orc said, looking back at the other Guild members, laughing and chatting jovially, punching each other in the necks.

"Oh!" The Orc said with a start. "I haven't introduced myself! I'm Grog."

He reached out for Eioffrey's hand and shook it.

"I'm Eioffrey," Eioffrey said.

They turned back to the fire. But they were soon joined by a man with a scar on his eye. He looked at them, and they looked back, but more scared.

"You two are rookies?" he finally said in a scratchy voice.

"Um, yeah," Eioffrey said.

"I'm guessing you two don't know the schedule," he said. "Training is tomorrow."

"Training?" Grog asked. "But we already...."

"Not *practice* training, *real* training!" the guy said. "We have three sections that everyone must participate in until they get a gold rank mission and complete it" he continued. "I'm getting off topic. Anyways, the first session is about being on a battlefield. We're not actually going to a battlefield. We're just doing a friendly game of paintball-up-the-rookie's-noses!"

He cackled and skipped off. Grog turned to Eioffrey.

"That didn't even make sense!" he exclaimed.

"Yeah, but he still is getting on my nerves," Eioffrey said. "His cackling gave me boosegumps."

"Goosebumps," Grog corrected.

"Right," Eioffrey said. "Alliance for paintball?"

"Sure, why not! I know you better than anyone here, and I barely know you at all!" Grog said, laughing.

Suddenly, a loud voice called out, "Lights out!" and every crystal's glow faded until the fire was the only source of light.

"Well, I think that means it's time to go to bed," Eioffrey said.

"Agreed," Grog said, getting up. "I'll leave the fire on so you can find your dwelling."

"Thanks," Eioffrey said. He walked up until he was at the door, then gave Grog the thumbs up as the light from the fire went out. Eioffrey changed into his pajamas and slid into bed like a missing piece of a puzzle and promptly fell asleep, knowing that tomorrow was going to be awesome.

Chapter 6

It was *not* awesome. Grog was awoken by a loud clanging, like pots and pans. And he should've known, because pots and pans were his *life*. But when he peered out the small slits he used as windows, he saw a giant bell ringing with an awful *CLANG, CLANG, CLANG*. There was the goblin from the previous night who was pulling on a rope, causing the ruckus. Apparently, no one else was fazed by this. It probably was the way they did this around here. The only other person besides Grog who was unprepared for the sudden noise was his neighbor, Eioffrey. He saw him stumbling out of his dwelling, rubbing his eyes ferociously and blinking like mad. Grog saw the other Guild members walking out and proceeding to a tunnel marked **Training Grounds**. He followed the crowd. Eventually he made his way to a large steel door with a large slab of rock next to it, like a miniature stage. Soon, the Guild Councillor from the previous night, Loram, stepped up and clapped his hands for attention. The chatter soon died down, and he cleared his throat.

"Guild members," he said. "I hope you're all ready to participate in some EleBall!"

Cheers erupted from the crowd, but Grog had no idea what the man was talking about.

"For those of you who are new, I'll explain the rules. You will be sorted into different teams of three, and you will be given a supply of EleBalls. You then will be placed around the arena, and your goal is to pummel the other teams with EleBalls and get their flag. Kind of like capture the flag, but more hardcore. The

EleBalls will have different effects depending on the color they emit. Any questions?"

Silence. Loram smiled.

"Then let the game begin!" he yelled, hitting a button on the wall and opening the door. The Guild members poured out into the stadium, each receiving a tube full of brightly colored balls, and tubes that looked like the fronts of vacuums. Grog got one. He was then ushered behind a small mountain that was about twenty feet tall. He was soon joined by Eioffrey, his friend from the night before.

"Hey, Eioffrey," Grog said. "You got dragged into this too?"

"Yeah," Eioffrey said, obviously out of it. "I feel too tired to really do anything, though."

Soon a man was brought to Eioffrey and Grog. Grog immediately recognized him. Ivan.

Once Ivan saw them, he flinched, developing a nasty twitch. Grog could tell Ivan was trying to change his mind, but a voice called over a loudspeaker, yelling:

"Alright, you all know what to do… now go get 'em!"

A loud buzzer sounded, and Ivan's defense mode must've locked on, because he immediately ducked and signaled for Eioffrey and Grog to do the same.

"Alright," said Ivan. "Here's the plan. The goal of the game is to capture at least five flags of five different teams. There are ten teams here, including us. Right now we have one flag: ours. I propose we get up to that pillar," he pointed at the highest spire of rock. "That way we have the high ground and can hit more people with EleBalls."

Without waiting for Eioffrey and Grog to agree, he took off to another rock. They followed, and soon another team wandered out into their field of vision. Ivan pointed at his tube, then at the team. Eioffrey and Grog got the message. *Hit them.* So they all readied their cannons, and swiftly shot the other team, leaving them coated in colorful muck. The one who was covered in the yellowish slime seemed to be paralyzed, while the other two, who were covered in a green speckled with purple, seemed as if they couldn't stop sneezing. More or less, they were restrained. Ivan took their flag, and led Eioffrey and Grog to a tunnel, where they met two other teams and did the same thing, taking those team's flags, too. Ivan eventually led them out the peak of the spire from before, and as they looked down, they could see everyone. Most teams had already been beaten, while other, more aggressive ones ran around, looking for a challenge. Grog slowly leaned down, aiming the cannon specifically at the man from the night before who had teased him and Eioffrey. He was leaning on a slab of rock, looking completely unconcerned. Grog shot an EleBall at him, covering him in a humiliating blue. He immediately teared up and started crying. Grog smirked.

"Come on!" Ivan said. "Let's get their flags!" They ran down the tunnel, but screeched to a stop when they saw a massive figure looming over the paralyzed players and taking the undeserved flags.

"Stay here," Ivan said. "I'll take care of him."

Ivan walked up to the giant man, aiming his cannon at him.

"Get away from those flags," Ivan said. "They're mine."

The big man laughed. "Presumptuous Ivan, always ruining my fun." He unhooked his own cannon and aimed it at Ivan.

Grog could see this was not going to turn out well. He looked at Eioffrey, pointing behind the big man. Eioffrey seemed to get the message.

"And where's your team?" the big man continued. "Oh-I bet they left you, just like Fryor," he laughed. Ivan's face contorted into a mix of a murderous glare and sadness.

"I'll make this easy on you," the man said. He shot an EleBall at Ivan, freezing him where he stood in a block of ice. The man laughed, but his victory did not last long. Eioffrey and Grog jumped out from their hiding spot behind the man, pelting him with so Many EleBalls that afterwards, they couldn't even see the man through the mix of colors. Grog stepped forward, grabbing the last flag they needed and raised all five in the air. A buzzer sounded, signaling the end of the match. Grog turned to Eioffrey, giving him a high-five. Officials swarmed in, gathering up Guild members and taking them off to get the EleBall essence off of them. Grog and Eioffrey were led out with a sense of accomplishment, but as Grog looked back at Ivan, the feeling died down. Who was Fryor? What happened to him?

Chapter 7

Ivan was humiliated. First, Devior, one of the rudest Guild members had insulted him to his face, and he didn't even fight back. Then he was frozen in a humiliating block of ice, and it stayed that way for at least two hours while some of the other Guild members tried melting the giant cube encasing his body with fire, but that didn't work. He had tried to act responsibly and bravely for his teammates, but now he was an idiot popsicle. When he was finally free, his body was numb, and he tried heading over to the sauna, which fortunately, was available. But once he got his body temperature back to its normal 27 degrees, he was summoned to the Boardroom for a test run with his new teammates. They had done so well in the EleBall game, that the council agreed to send them to retrieve a cargo from Echolocation Air Station, the Blimp port of the Northern continent. He, Eioffrey, and Grog were sent there on a blimp soon after. When they got to Reverb Port, though, there were gates surrounding the place. Ivan walked up to someone who looked like he was in charge.

"What's happening here?" he asked.

The man turned to him. "Pirates," he said. He apparently was worried. Ivan raised an eyebrow.

"This much for pirates? Where are they?" he asked.

The man pointed to the large building that stood on the edge of Reverb Port.

"In there," he said. "Why?"

"Because we're gonna take them out," Ivan said, cracking his knuckles.

The man sighed. "Well, don't say I didn't warn you. These guys have some *Big Gear*, if you know what I mean."

Ivan just nodded. He stepped over the gate, followed by Eioffrey and Grog. When they opened the door to the building, they immediately saw the problem. In the middle of the room was a giant Mecha-Suit with a man inside. Several pipes sprouted from the neck point, and Grog gasped.

"What?" Ivan whispered.

"I know that kind of armor!" Grog whispered back.

Ivan looked at him sceptically. "Really?" he said.

"Yeah!" Grog said. "I'm from Orkro Kingdom! That suit of armor is something that some of the disadvantaged wear to battle, to make themselves stronger! It's called Ultra Armor 7! I know all the weak points! It was probably stolen!"

Ivan sighed. "Very well, lead the way."

"Okay," Grog said. "I'm gonna try and distract him, and you two take out the legs, tying them together might be best. Then, when he tries to walk, he'll fall over. My bet is that there's a small guy in there."

Ivan and Eioffrey nodded. Ivan led Eioffrey outback, while Grog caught the pirate's attention. As Ivan and Eioffrey were going around the building, Ivan asked Eioffrey something.

"What do you have?"

Eioffrey turned to him in confusion.

"Grog said we needed to tie his legs together. Do you have any rope?"

"Um, no."

Ivan groaned. "Neither do I. Great. *Real* great."

"Oh!" Eioffrey said. He pulled out his pendant.

Ivan looked at the pendant, then Eioffrey. He raised an eyebrow. "What're you going to do with that?"

"Grab at his legs and pull them backwards!" Eioffrey said, like it was the most obvious thing ever. Ivan sighed, and they snuck in through the **staff only** door. Eventually they got to the front where Grog was giving a pep talk to the pirate about why he shouldn't be a pirate. But Ivan could see that the pirate wasn't buying it, fidgeting and looking from side to side like he was expecting something to happen.

"Quickly," Ivan said. "While he's distracted."

Eioffrey shot out a beam of energy and grasped the robotic bodysuit's legs and attempted to pull backwards. But it didn't even budge, and it definitely caught the pirate's attention. His head swiveled around, and Ivan got a first good look at him. He wore a steel helmet tipped with electric rods, goggles that covered his eyes, and a gas mask. So Ivan couldn't make out the exact details. He seemed half surprised, half expecting this to happen. He looked down at the essence encasing his legs, and simply shot an electric current down his leg and onto Eioffrey, shocking him. The magic recoiled, and Eioffrey crumpled to the ground. Ivan gasped, pulling out his sword and charging at the pirate and grasped onto the torso of the suit. The pirate pressed another button, and the torso started spinning around like an out-of-control merry-go-round. Eventually Ivan lost his grip and was flung like a used dish cloth against the wall, falling to the ground. The pirate and his suit approached him, charging up one of its hands to shock Ivan, but suddenly, a frying pan flew up and knocked the suit behind the knees, causing it to crumple. Ivan looked up and saw that Grog had thrown the cooking tool. The pirate stepped out, flailing around. Grog ran up to him, punching him in the head and knocking him out cold. He crumpled to the ground, and Grog came over to help Ivan and Eioffrey up.

"Thanks," Ivan said. "I think he would've gotten me."

Grog chuckled. 'It's funny that I was supposed to be the distraction, but it ended up being you guys!"

Ivan had to admit that he had a point. After Eioffrey was back awake, they went over to the pirate, who was still unconscious.

"Time to see who the pirate is," Ivan said, reaching out to grasp the helmet. He yanked it off, and gasped.

It was Loram.

Chapter 8

Eioffrey was both worried and shocked. When he, Ivan and Grog had brought the unconscious Loram to the Guildmaster, his face contorted and his body tightened. He stayed like that for about ten minutes before saying anything. He then took in a deep breath, and let it out. He turned to Ivan.

"And he was operating a stolen war suit? Headgear and all?"

"Yes," Ivan said. "The goggles and mask covered up his face, so he probably didn't want to be seen."

The Guildmaster started fingering a rock in his hands. "Ivan, had he been acting suspicious lately?"

"Well," Ivan said. "He asked me to stand guard for a meeting a few days ago. And he paid me this," he pulled out a large coin out of a small pocket in his breastplate. The Guildmaster took it and examined it.

"This," he said. "Is…."

"A wandering coin?" Ivan interrupted.

The Guildmaster turned to him with a look of shock on his face. "How did you know that?"

"He kind of told me," Ivan said.

"Do you know how it works?" the Guildmaster inquired.

Ivan for once was silent. The Guildmaster took the coin and started pulling on the top. It snapped off, and he pulled something out. It was red, and it pulsed with an uneasy light.

"A tracking device," the Guildmaster said. He looked at Loram. Suddenly, he leapt forward and slapped the man across the face, waking him up immediately. Loram stuttered and looked over at the Guildmaster. He was still in a state of unconsciousness, but when he saw the scarlet face looming over him, he quickly recovered. The Guildmaster put on a disturbing, cracked smile.

"Loram," he muttered. "Mind telling us about your little adventure? About *this?*" he pulled out the coin.

Loram looked at the coin, then at the Guildmaster. He cracked a smirk.

"So you've figured it out?" he asked. "I was wondering when you would."

"So you're a pirate now?" the Guildmaster yelled.

"It's much more than that, sir," Loram said. "Me and most of the other Councillors have wanted more than just silly quests and errands. We plan to get more cash soon, to make up for wasted days," he laughed.

"You're going to tell me everything," the Guildmaster said. "Everything."

Loram smiled. "No, I'm not. You always fail to see the bigger picture, Julius."

Suddenly, he brought out a small object from his sleeve, dropping it on the ground, causing it to break and send up a fume of smoke. When the mist cleared, he had disappeared. The door was swinging open, and outside lay a few confused looking people. The Guildmaster shook ferociously, his eyes lit with rage. He suddenly pounded his fist on the table, snapping it in half. Eioffrey backed up immediately, surprised and scared by what the Guildmaster was doing. After composing himself, the Guildmaster turned to Ivan.

"Tell me, who else was in this *meeting?*"

Ivan and the Guildmaster went around the Guild, to find the other traitorous Councillors. But when they arrived at the homes, they were nowhere to be found. Once they had returned, the Guildmaster was furious. He had Grog put up wanted posters all over the city, while Ivan and Eioffrey were excused. Ivan decided to lead Eioffrey to Nightshade Inn and take it easy. Ivan ordered Eioffrey some juice, and they sat silently, not speaking a word. But soon, a man ran in, breathing heavily.

"They're coming!" he yelled.

Everyone in the tavern stared at the man blankly.

"Pirates!" he repeated. "They're coming! Look outside for yourself!"

Everyone in Nightshade Inn ran out to look. Sure enough, giant ships were emerging from the clouds, like dragons coming out of their caves. Ivan turned to the man.

"You need to tell the Guild!" he said.

"I already did!" the man said. "The Guildmaster said he was expecting something like this to happen, but I didn't know what he meant!"

Eloffrey turned to Ivan with a worried expression on his face. Ivan looked back.

"Don't worry, kid. We'll be fine. Just need help from an old friend."

Ivan led Eioffrey to a run-down cottage on the edge of Guidway City. He knocked on the door, and a crusty voice called out.

"Come in."

Ivan took Eioffrey inside, where he saw an old man with grey hair and a withering moustache. He lay slumped on a couch, with several boxes of once-packaged food piled on the floor. His right eye was as grey as his hair, and it radiated a dark energy.

"Hey, Fryor," Ivan said. "I'm afraid we have some bad news."

Fryor looked confused. "Did Tortel's Market run out of the pork balls?"

"No, nothing like that. This is much worse. Pirates are invading Guidway City."

Fryor looked taken aback. "So you know what you must do!"

"I know, but fighting pirates was the one thing you wanted to do most! I wanted you to have this chance!"

Fryor smiled a sad smile. "Ivan," he said. "Do you think a man like me can take on pirates right now? I've been carrying this disease around for so long that I don't think I'd even be able to move. This is up to you."

Ivan nodded. He got up and walked out the door. Eioffrey followed, but he could tell that what Fryor had was not a disease. It was a curse.

Chapter 9

Grog had been warned of the arrival of the pirates from the moment he heard a man yelling: "Pirates! Pirates ARE COMING! WE'RE ALL DOOMED!" at the top of his lungs. Grog caught him by the shoulder.

"Just a tip," he said. "Thanks for warning us. But this isn't a contest to see how many people you can make go deaf."

The man nodded ferociously and kept running, now yelling at a more appropriate volume. Grog ran to the Guild, where he bumped into Ivan and Eioffrey. Together they made their way down into the Guild. When they got there, they saw the Guildmaster and all the other members had gathered in the dining hall. Grog was astonished.

"What are all you doing?" he yelled. "We need to fight the pirates!"

The rude Guild member turned to them and said:

"Did you see how many ships there are? There's no way we can fight them all. We're just waiting out here. Peri won't let them in."

"But what about the City?" Grog said. "They're defenseless! We need to protect them! Are you guys just going to wait until they come knocking?"

Suddenly a loud, suffocating *THUD* reverberated above them as dirt and chunks of rocks fell from the ceiling. Grog looked at the crowd.

"Well, I don't want to say I told you...." he said.

"Not to worry," another Guild member said. "Peri will keep them off."

There was a scream from above, and it sounded distinctly like a telescope being throttled.

"I stand corrected," the man muttered.

"We need to defend the city, or there won't *be* a city to defend!" Grog said. "Who's with me?"

Behind him, Eioffrey and Ivan raised their hands. No other hands went up. Grog groaned.

"Fine. I guess we'll do this by ourselves," he said and headed out the tunnels to the first floor, followed by Ivan and Eioffrey. But they immediately ran into three pirates who had just come down on the platinum disc, brandishing swords. He and Ivan knocked them to the ground, stealing their swords and handed one to Eioffrey. They shot up the platinum panel and realized that only one ship had docked at the mountain. At the front of the ship lay Peri, but he appeared to have been smashed into the ground very violently.

"Peri!" Eioffrey cried. "What happened to you?"

The periscope struggled to talk. "They surprised me. If I had seen 'em coming, I woulda knocked their socks off."

Ivan rolled his eyes. "Sure, Peri."

"We'll help you as soon as we take care of the pirates," Grog said.

Peri sighed. "Fine. But you don't know what it feels like to be smashed into the ground!"

The other ships were headed towards the city, and that could only be bad news. The gate was still open, so they all went inside. They encountered about ten more pirates, fighting them off and tying them up. Eventually they made their way to the front of the ship, where a pirate was lazily eating a sandwich (stolen, probably). Ivan immediately jumped up, putting the guy in a chokehold. As he carried him off, Grog took control of the ship. He was no expert, but he could figure out which pedal was 'Go' and how to steer pretty quickly. Once Ivan got back, Grog told them his plan.

"I'm going to try and ram this ship into the others," he said. "Hopefully it will puncture them, and none will be left."

Grog stomped on the 'Go' pedal, and steered the ship towards the others. But when they got closer, Grog realized that they were coated in a thick layer of steel, making them impenetrable. Grog turned to Ivan and Eioffrey frantically.

"We need to get off this ship!" he yelled, and dashed out of the control room. He was soon followed by Eioffrey and Ivan, and they headed to the very top of the ship. But when Eioffrey looked over the side, he looked like he would be sick. Grog had started to doubt his plan right as the prow of the ship rammed into the side of another. It didn't puncture it, but it did knock it over, turning it 180 degrees. Unfortunately, that caused the ship that they were on to lurch forward, forcing Ivan to grab both of them and leap over the chasm that expanded below them. He landed on the other ship, and drew out his sword. The bottom of the ship was unprotected, so he ran his blade through it, leaving a giant rip through it.

"Jump to the next one!" Ivan yelled. "I'll deal with this one!"

Grog wasn't as good at jumping as Ivan was, but he grabbed Eioffrey and jumped to the next ship, almost not making it. Eioffrey shot out a beam of light from his pendant, proceeding to tear the bottom of the ship to shreds. Grog turned to the last one, which just so happened to be the biggest. Just his luck. He sprung to it, and landed just on the side of the enormous ship. He slipped, clutching a loose metal plate. He pulled himself up and made his way into the ship. He wandered through the hallways, full of exhaust pipes and machines, and eventually made his way to the control room, which was much larger than the ones in the other ships. There were rows of seats on the sides for people to manage the cannons and a giant glass window at the front where the steering wheel was. And at the steering wheel was Loram, dressed in a captain's hat and a dark robe. When he heard Grog come in, he turned around in shock, then the shock turned into a wide grin.

"Oh no," he said in a baby voice. "The pwecious wittle hewoes are here to ruin my plan! Oh, how sad!"

He smiled and pressed a button. A giant cage fell from the ceiling, encasing Grog. He looked at it in confusion.

"How much did you pay to make this?" he asked.

"Shut up!" Loram yelled. "At any rate, you can enjoy watching me pillage and destroy Guildway City! Maybe if you're a good boy I'll even let you live!"

Grog hated being called a 'good boy.' His rage powered him, and his teeth locked onto the steel bars. He started gnawing on them, ripping them apart. Loram turned to him in shock.

"What the...? You aren't supposed to be able to do that!" he yelled with a hint of fear in his tone.

"Listen, buddy," Grog said. "I've eaten blocks of cheese tougher than these bars."

He promptly whacked Loram upside the head. He crumpled to the floor, and Grog picked him up, walking off. But suddenly the ship started leaning right toward Guidway City, and Grog realized that Loram had been steering the thing. He took one of the metal bars he had ripped off and threw it at the steering wheel, knocking it left and away from Guidway City. Unfortunately, they started heading towards some distant mountains instead. So Grog ran out of the ship with Loram still clutched in his hands. He found the exit and took a daring jump. Thirty feet off the ground wasn't too much, right? Thankfully, the place they were soaring above was covered in trees, otherwise they might have not survived. Grog fell into some trees, dropping Loram. He hit his head on the ground and knocked himself out. When he awoke, he saw Ivan and Eioffrey looking at him. He looked at his surroundings and realized from the glowing crystals that he was in the Guild.

"Are you okay?" Eioffrey asked.

"I-I think so," Grog said. "Where's Loram?"

Ivan twitched. "That little sack of weasels scampered away before we got there. He's still loose."

"But what matters is that you're alright," Eioffrey said. He laid his hand on Grog's.

Grog patted him on the back. Suddenly a man dashed into the room, out of breath.

"Ivan!" he said. He leaned on the wall. He must have been running for a while.

Ivan turned to him. "What is it? Did they find Loram?"

"No," the man said, his worried expression intensifying. "It's Fryor."

Chapter 10

Ivan was running frantically. When he had heard the news about Fryor, he immediately took off. If something was wrong with his teacher, his father figure, he would put the rest of the world behind him. He dashed down the stairs of the Guidway Guild, past Nightshade Inn, and eventually to the cottage, where several officers stood guard.

"Let me in!" Ivan demanded.

"Sorry, no can do," the officer said. "I've got strict orders that no one is allowed inside."

"Listen here, buddy," Ivan said, grabbing the front of the man's shirt and lifting him up. "That's my father figure in there. He means everything to me, and NO ONE is going to stop me from seeing him."

He dropped the guard, who was whimpering and ran to the entrance. He opened the door and gasped in horror. Fryor was sitting on the couch as usual, but now large, gray, lifeless vines sprouted from his left eye and were wrapping around his body. Ivan ran towards him. Fryor was barely able to look back at him.

"Fryor!" Ivan said. "What happened to you?"

"It's the disease," he choked, the vines tightening. "It's getting stronger."

"D-don't worry!" Ivan said. He unsheathed his sword and aimed at the vines. But Fryor held out his hand.

"No, Ivan."

"But we need to get these off of you!" He was starting to get teary-eyed.

"Ivan," Fryor said. "We can't stop this from happening. I've known what fate had in store for me a long time ago. And I think we both know that I can't be around forever."

Ivan sniffled. "But I need to help...."

"Ivan," Fryor said, putting his hand up to Ivan's cheek. The vines tightened around Fryor. "You can't help me. I was destined for this. I want you to know that I will always treasure our moments we had together. You are my legacy. I love you."

Ivan was crying now. "I-I love you too, F-Fryor."

"Good, good...," Fryor said, the vines almost encasing his body. "Keep an eye on those friends of yours," he smiled.

His blue right eye faded into a murky gray. The vines recoiled, and his head slumped. Ivan stood back.

He was dead.

Epilogue

Five weeks later, Eioffrey, Grog and Ivan had cleaned out the old cottage, sweeping up the dust from the floor and replacing floor boards. After they had cleaned up, they all felt like it should have been done a long time ago. Grog and Eioffrey were invited to live there with Ivan and made home for themselves in one of the unused rooms. Ivan slept in Fryor's room, which hadn't occupied anyone in it for at least a year. Aside from that, after single handedly (or maybe triple handedly) defeating three airships and a crew of pirates, were all given a gold rank. There were other changes in the Guild. The Guildmaster decided that he and he alone would be in charge, no one else. The crew of pirates, who consisted of the other Guild councillors and some other pirates were locked away, in a secret prison that almost no one knew the location of. At the cottage, Ivan lay awake in the midst of the night. Fryor's funeral was tomorrow, and everyone at the Guild was requested to come.

"Ivan?"

Ivan looked up. He had been staring into his pint of beer for five minutes and the foam was starting to evaporate. He chugged it down and slammed it back onto the table. Eioffrey was looking at him with a concerned expression on his face.

"Are you alright?" Grog asked. "The funeral is in ten minutes. Should we head over?"

"Sure," was all Ivan said. They walked out of Nightshade Inn, down the twisting road and into the Guidway Guild. They walked up the stairs, where some dwarves were repairing Peri's hole. The periscope lay on the ground, and Ivan saw that he was apparently some kind of squid or something, stuck inside the periscope, and could talk. A talking squid stuck in a periscope.

"Nice tentacles." Grog said.

"Thank you." Peri replied. If he could look smug, he definitely did now.

They continued up their way, to the Platinum disc and shot down to the lowest level of the Guild, where the funeral would be held. They passed the rows of Guild members, some with sad expressions, others who were trying to look sad and failing. At the very front, the coffin lay flat, ready to be buried in the ground. Ivan took one last look at the man who had truly raised him, and signaled that they could bury him. Four men walked up to the coffin and gently laid it into the ground. They then took Fryor's sword, placing it on top of the coffin. They heaved up some shovels and started piling dirt on it, encasing it completely. The funeral finished, and everyone was allowed to go home. Ivan just stayed there, never wanting to leave the coffin. But he felt Eioffrey and Grog's eyes on him, and he chose to leave. When they got back to the cottage, Eioffrey fell down onto the couch from exhaustion, his little feet could only walk so far. Ivan sat next to him, followed by Grog. Ivan looked at them both.

"You know," he said. "I sure am lucky to end up with teammates like you."

"You're lucky?" Eioffrey said. "We're the lucky ones to end up with a leader like you!"

"Ditto," Grog said, pulling them both into a bear hug. Ivan struggled for a minute, but obliged to it after a few seconds. He sighed, looking out the window at the starry night, at a new sky, at a new life.

"I sure wonder what the future has in store for us..."

Extras

Guidway Guild

Guild members:

Ivan - #15, Team Amber - Age: 21 - Species: Human

Eioffrey - #16, Team Amber - Age: 10 - Species: Human

Grog - #17, Team Amber - Age: 25 - Species: Orc

Teryl - #18, Team Tanzanite - Age: 190 - Species: elf

Devior - #19, Team Tanzanite - Age: 35 - Species: dwarf

Arsley - #20, Team Tanzanite - Age: 37 - Species: Human

Jon - #10, Team Ruby - 36 - Species: Orc

Jorah - #11, Team Ruby - 36 - Species: Orc

Francis - #12, Team Ruby - 36 - Species: Orc

Varnian - #5, Team Emerald - Age: 56 - Species: Human

Uruik - #6, Team Emerald - Age: possibly as old as creation itself - Species: Shadow being

Salmon - #7, Team Emerald - Age: 13 - Species: Half-breed

Brutus - #13, Team Morganite - Age: 80 - Species: Orc

Calepryen - #2, Team Zircon - Age: 60 - Species: Human

Soravv - #3, Team Zircon - Age: 345 - Species: elf

Torundous - #4, Team Zircon - Age: 124 - Species: Half-breed

Fryor - #14, Team Amber, previously Team Morganite - Age: 58 - Species: Human

Guild Staff:

Peri - Watchman - Age: Uknown - Species: Mimic

Regamore - Chef and Alarm Clock - Age: 45 - Species: goblin

Po - 1st Janitor - Age: 2 - Species: Imp

Mo - 2nd Janitor - Age: 2 - Species: Imp

Wo - 3rd Janitor - Age: 2 - Species: Imp

Julius Stoneseeker - Guildmaster - Age: 64 - Species: Human

Guidway City

Locations:

Guidway Guild
Town Square
Moonset Hills
Nightshade Inn
Market
Fields
Fryor's Cottage
Village

Notable Citizens:

Billy the Bartender - Bartender of Nightshade Inn - Age: 54 -
Species: Human

Old Flo - Maid for hire - Age: 93 - Species: Human

Tortel - Chef/Butcher - Age: 37 - Species: Half-breed

Alister - Fortune Teller - Age: 245 - Species: elf

Ms. Weller - Citizen - Age: 64 - Species: Human

Drugle - Town Idiot - Age: Unknown - Species: Ogre

Outlaws:

Loram Whichseker - Crime: Piratry and Betrayal - Status: Loose

Louis Berrybomb - Crime: Piratry and Betrayal - Status: Captured

Everglen Sprouts - Crime: Piratry and Betrayal - Status: Captured

Balious Gergen - Crime: Piratry and Betrayal - Status: Captured

Indigo Nitherheim - Crime: Thievery - Status: Captured

Vance Skenoughner - Crime: Attempted human sacrifice and destruction towards a species - Status: Escaped/Loose

Alexandra Stoneseeker - Crime: Unknown - Status: Missing

Pronunciations:

Ivan
(EYE-van)

Eioffrey
(EEY-off-for-ey)

Grog
(GR-og)

Guidway City
(GUIDE-way si-tee)

Bludmud cave
(Blood-MUD ca-yve)

Nightshade Inn
(NYTE-shayd in)

Barvey
(BAR-vey)

Iris

(IY-riss)

Oble
(AH-bole)

Vance
(VAN-s)

Vanilla
(VAN-ill-a)

Manti
(MON-tee)

Aro
(AR-o)

Fryor
(FRY-or)

Patapata Town
(PATA-pata Town)

About Author & Illustrator Matthew Randolph

Matthew Randolph lives in the Bay Area of California with his family and two cats, Loki and Cleopatra. His hobbies are drawing, writing, programming on Scratch, and eating lasagna. Lots of lasagna. He plans to continue writing *Call To A Quest* in the future.